SALSA MAGIC

SalsaMagic

Letisha Marrero

LQ

LEVINE QUERIDO

MONTCLAIR · AMSTERDAM · HOBOKEN

This is an Arthur A. Levine book
Published by Levine Querido

LQ

LEVINE QUERIDO

www.levinequerido.com • info@levinequerido.com

Levine Querido is distributed by Chronicle Books, LLC

Library of Congress Control Number: 2023932260
ISBN 978-1-64614-260-6

Printed and bound in China

Published in August 2023
First Printing

For Jaylen

Contents

SALSA MAGIC

Chapter 1

Welcome to Café Taza

"Ay, sí . . . New Yorkers and their weekend brunches," Abuela Chacha says, standing in the doorway, her face basking in the late summer Sunday morning rays. New York City is sticky and hot-hot-hot in August, but the humidity hasn't totally kicked in yet. Abuela turns around to admire the interior of the small but vibrant Café Taza, with its Caribbean blue and sunflower yellow walls, as if it were her vast queendom.

"Excuse me, Abuela," I say as I groggily walk past her into the family-owned restaurant and head to the coffee station behind the red formica counter. Carajo, I could sure use a cafecito this morning! But Mami thinks that, at thirteen, I'm too young to start drinking coffee. I am wearing jeggings, a turquoise tee, and a purple zip-up hoodie, and some matching two-tone kicks on my size-eleven feet. My rizos are snatched up in a messy bun, and tucked under my arm is my soccer ball—for later.

Abuela follows me to the espresso machine behind the counter to make her own café con leche. "Every Saturday and Sunday, it's like some pagan ritual for these eepsters to cleanse their sinful spirits from the night before with coffee, eggs, and salchicha." She laughs as she lightly foams the milk.

I giggle at the way she says "hipsters." I sidle up behind her and give her a backwards hug.

Abuela Chacha is petite but mighty—with that certain soft fullness around the middle that grandmothers have to make their nietos feel safe and warm. But she still has these killer dancer's legs—and the woman knows how to work them. Abuela always wears above-the-knee skirts and dresses or capri pants to flaunt "lo que Dios me dio."

Saturdays and Sundays are usually our busiest days—one, for the coffee, two, for a slammin' plate of huevos rancheros or panqueques. Café Taza is a family business in every sense of the word, so everybody has to pitch in—especially on weekends, especially during the summer. It's kind of a drag, and probably against some of the city's child labor laws, but we're all so used to it that there is no other way to live for us. Plus, who can afford summer camp? So whenever we aren't at school (or soccer practice for me), you can usually find three generations of Calderones at Café Taza in Fort Greene, Brooklyn, serving up mofongo, sandwiches de pernil, and—Brooklyn's best-kept secret—the most epic cafés con leche in the borough.

"Dos cafés," Tio Fausto barks in my general direction.

That's my cue. Abuela's third-born but first male, Tio Fausto, runs the front of the house. He's a burly, surly man with bushy eyebrows that scowl easily, a head full of black curls, and a sturdy, confident gait. The man loves his money—er, I mean, customers—whom he is almost too happy to oblige. "Right this way," he says sweetly as he ushers a couple to a two-top in the corner. A real Jekyll and Hyde, that one.

Yawning, I bend over to tuck my soccer ball into a shelf underneath the counter, put on an apron, empty the used coffee grounds from one of the espresso machines, scoop and pack the fresh coffee into the filter, and fire up another cup for the next customer. I'm pretty good at it, which is why I'm the token barista at the café. Occasionally, I feel the need to taste my foamy creation, so I'm already planning when I could sneak one. Since Mami's domain is in the kitchen, I can manage to take a few forbidden sips every once in a while. I just have to watch out for the swinging door, in case she walks into the dining room to get her own cafecito.

I yawn again as I steam the milk in the stainless steel frother. I didn't get a lot of sleep last night. I had one of my crazy dreams again. They're happening more often now. I've always been one to daydream, but these "awake dreams" are weird, and my night dreams are even trippier. Sometimes it feels like déjà vu, like I walk into a place that feels mad familiar even though I've never been there before. Or sometimes, I feel someone watching over me, like a spirit.

I saw that woman in my dreams again last night. (More on that later. The brunch rush is heating up now . . .)

Just at the exact moment I dare to put my lips to a small to-go cup filled with the extra coffee, I hear the kitchen door swing open. Carajo! Mami sticks her head out, as if just to bust me, and says quietly but firmly, "Maya Beatriz, no," giving me el mal ojo, the evil eye.

I put the coffee cup down and turn to sigh wistfully in defeat. My morning jolt will have to wait. On the other side of the counter, a tall, slender, but muscular woman with faded pink hair, a nose ring, bra top, and yoga pants, carrying a rolled-up mat asks me, "Excuse me, miss. One coffee, please. Do you have nonfat milk?"

Uh oh. That's usually Abuelo's cue to go off. "¿Leche sin grasa? ¿Y pa' qué?" he asks as he walks over from the other side of the counter.

Before el viejito can grouse any more, I hold my arm out to intercept his oncoming rant. "Yes ma'am, I'll make you one."

Actually, I totally agree with Abuelo: If you don't use whole milk, the foam doesn't come out right. The consistency isn't right. The color of the coffee isn't right. The taste isn't right. But "skinny" is how the blanquitos who have swarmed into the neighborhood like their coffee. Or worse, with soy milk (I am milk?) or almond milk. But we Nuyoricans need their business to stay afloat. In this cut-throat restaurant business, it is either change or die. But Abuelo draws the line at oat milk. "¿Leche de avena? ¿¿¿Cómo es posible???"

After I'm done, he goes to the espresso machine, foams the whole milk, and makes another cup the "proper way." Then he holds up the back of his light brown hand as evidence. "¿Lo ves? Café con leche is sup-posed to be the color of my skin!"

"Got it, Abuelo," I say, looking down and patting his balding head that's surrounded by a halo of wiry silver tufts.

"Dos cafés for Table Three!" shouts Tio Fausto as he zips past the counter.

Even though Tio Fausto is the third youngest in the Calderon family, he's the only son, so he holds special status as the head of the family. (Because viva la patriarchy, or something.) His wife, Titi Julia, a former accountant, pleasantly oversees the register and the finances. Mami, mis abuelos' second-eldest daughter, is in charge of the kitchen. The eldest, my Titi Dolores, lives in California, unfortunately. She and her family being three thousand miles away goes against everything a close-knit Latine family is supposed to be. I don't get to see my cousins Taina and Tommy very often, and we're all so close in age, it would be fun if we were all together. But I guess that's what happens when you fall in love with a Hollywood TV producer—you move to Los Angeles.

"Behind," Trini says as she scooches by me and Abuelo, balancing three plates of hot food. The smells are mind-melding—that heady garlic, green pepper, tomato, and onion combo called sofrito goes a long, wonderful way.

Beautiful Trinidad, or Trini, is the waitress, and Abuela's youngest child. She almost counts as one of us cousins, because at nineteen, she's sandwiched in between generations. She's cool, pretty, and always stylish with the bomb blowout and the latest fashions. But she's like, *sooo* into herself. Even though Trini is really my tía, I refuse to call her that, since she is only like, six years and seven months older than me. So, she's more like what we call a tía sister cousin.

But every Latine family I know has some sort of odd-ball relation—you know, like a few branches are missing off their family tree. For example, I have my traditional cousins, like Tio Fausto and Titi Julia's kids: Inez, Minerva, and Erasmo—aka Ini, Mini, and Mo—twin twelve-year-old girls who imagine they're in a girl band, and their six-year-old impish brother, who keep everyone on their toes. But I also have relatives who are, like, sixty years old, who are actually my third or fourth cousins and whom I call tío or tía. It's a respect thing.

Trini slinks up to the counter, fluffs her hair, and grabs two cafés con leche.

"Hottie at Table Eight!" she whispers as she turns on her heels to deliver the cups to Table Three.

Salma, my eleven-year-old sister and the complete opposite of me in every way, stops wiping Table Six down, turns around, and adjusts her glasses to get a clearer glimpse. In the corner booth by the kitchen, Ini and Mini look up from their game of Uno with Mo (someone has to keep him entertained). See, Trini has this game called "Spot the Hottie," where we all have to identify whatever rando good-looking man enters the café. What makes it worse is that she usually gets the fine dude's attention because she's filled out in all the right places—you know, where all the men in the café drool over her big nalgas as she walks away. "Bien mujer," everyone has been telling Trini ever since her quinceañera. And now that she's in college, all this womanhood stuff is going straight to her head. Plus, she's totally boy crazy. I can't relate. Oscar from the bodega next door has had a crush on Trini since she was my age, and she milks that for all that it's worth—which usually translates into a free ice tea, or a bag of chicharrones, a single rose, or something else that screams regular degular yet romantic.

Sometimes, like just now, I see Trini throw in an extra hip-sway, hoping for that extra tip. Salma and I just roll our eyes, while Tio Fausto, Trini's older brother, looks ready to fight somebody.

Meanwhile, Chacha and Chucho Calderon, mis abuelos, keep the customers happy. Wherever they go, Chacha and Chucho steal the show. O sea, they *are* the show. And here they go . . .

"Querida," Abuelo Chucho starts in after stepping inside from his game of sidewalk dominos.

"Sí, mi amor," Abuela Chacha calls from the other side of the café.

"Bésame," he says suggestively. The two make sweeping arm gestures as they slowly walk gracefully toward another. Then he croons, "Bésame mucho . . ." taking Chacha into his arms. Then, the couple begins to dance romantically and harmonize the famous torch song while gazing into each other's eyes. The customers look up from their heaping brunch plates and smile at their impromptu performance. A few even clap.

The still-spry, still-in-love couple is also known for breaking out into dance in the restaurant aisles with a salsa or bachata routine and are quick to remind people that they are the former salsa dancing king and queen of Bayamón, Puerto Rico. Together, they are magical.

My grandparents came to New York City in the late seventies, when they were young and the Latin jazz scene was really on and poppin'. Abuela and Abuelo always regale us (and anyone who'll listen) with stories from their colorful past about how they used to hang with legendary salsa musicians, like Tito Puente, Celia Cruz, and Johnny Pacheco, and the café's walls are decorated with framed photographs to back it up.

"Celia's husband Pedro was so devoted to her. He never left her side. ¡Qué romántico!" Abuela tells the yoga-mat-toting blanquita with pink hair, who is lingering with her café con leche and admiring Celia's photo.

Anytime anyone comes within a foot of the photo of Johnny Pacheco, Abuelo says, "That Johnny owed me money! May he rest in peace."

See, in the early 1980s, they bought a building and opened Club Coco, and it became, like, *the* place to dance and be seen.

"Only the Copa was more famous because it was bigger and in midtown Manhattan, instead of way out in Brooklyn," Abuelo Chucho likes to brag to customers.

But when mambo and Latin jazz cooled off, Chacha and Chucho were forced to close the club. Then, after 9/11, my Tio Fausto, a former Wall Streeter, came up with the idea of turning the storefront space into a restaurant and converting the top floor into a trio of rentable apartments, for extra money.

I know from Abuelo Chucho's whispering that the café's popularity has slowed down some since I was born. Then, after the coronavirus, the restaurant took a big hit. Tio Fausto had to shut everything down during the pandemic. When the mayor said that restaurants could open again, we did takeout orders to keep us afloat, but it wasn't enough. It's been rough, but now that the restaurant has reopened, things are getting better—pero slowly.

One day, I asked Tio Fausto if Abuelo's grumblings are something to be worried about. My uncle says a lot of it is due to gentrification, which means the neighborhood is changing—and our main clientele is dwindling, because the new neighbors prefer the trendy restaurants over the local hangout spots. What used to be a working-class Black and Latino neighborhood has morphed into mostly rich, white professionals, who buy up brownstones and storefronts and renovate them into something unrecognizable. As a result, the rents have gone up, driving families who have lived in Brooklyn for decades to find cheaper rent elsewhere. And prices for everything else have skyrocketed. For example, instead of just having Jorge and his son Oscar's corner bodega to satisfy your basic needs, there are shops where you can buy expensive wine, gourmet cheese, imported coffee, bubble tea, and artisan jewelry—which I guess is another word for expensive, based on the price tags I see in the window display. And, of course, the Starbucks every three blocks doesn't help business either.

One thing about Puerto Ricans, though: We are a proud people who stay true to ourselves and do not give up—so the Calderones continue to center Café Taza around Mami's authentic criollo recipes. Mami may not say much, but from a young age, she could cook her pompis off. Mis abuelos always say they never know how they conceived such a reserved child as my mom. Then again, maybe they shouldn't have named their daughter Soledad (it's Spanish for loneliness).

Watching Mami work is a trip. She goes completely by feel—rubbing the oregano between her thumb and forefinger and taking a deep whiff before putting it in the cast-iron pan. Grinding the garlic in the mortar and pestle as if she is pressing each clove back into the earth itself. Chopping the onions and letting her salty tears fall freely, not even stopping to wipe them away. Coring the seedy center of each green pepper with her fingers. Peeling the delicate ribbons of skin off the tomatoes.

Steam rises as she sautés everything together into a savory pulp, creating vats of sofrito, the spicy tomato-based sauce that seasons almost every criollo dish. When the spices mix together and waft to the ceiling, it is intoxicating—almost like magic. In fact, Mami is so secretive about her recipes, the family calls her cooking "salsa magic."

Abuela's side of the family is known as Los Locos—as Trini, who is always doling out the bochinche, tells us. There is the pyromaniac, the kleptomaniac, the alcoholic, the hypochondriac. There's also the schizophrenic—the late Tia Cuca who swore she was married to Tito Puente, the famous Puerto Rican drummer and bandleader, and claimed she was his backup singer. And then, of course, there is the witch: Abuela's older sister, who still lives on the island. I don't know much about her, because she is estranged from the family and no one is supposed to mention her. All I've heard from Trini is that she is rumored to cast spells and sacrifice chickens and stuff.

I don't like the idea that my great aunt, whom I've never met, is in Puerto Rico all by herself, while the rest of us are here in Brooklyn. It's almost as bad as Titi Dolores and my cousins being in California. We're supposed to be a tight-knit family, and this vieja is all alone on an island. And also because, the truth is, sometimes I wonder if I am a little "loca" myself. Those dreams I have . . .

sometimes they feel more real to me than serving up cafés con leche at Café Taza or dribbling the ball on the soccer pitch. And what scares me even more than the dreams is that I can never tell anyone in my family about them, ever. I can imagine the disappointed look on Abuela Chacha's face, the sound of Abuelo's scoffing, and Mami's concerned eyebrows. Being dismissed. And then, after that, the loneliness.

Chapter 2

The Witch Who Would Live Above the Café

IN THE LATE MORNING, the clouds start to hover, and by noon, it is raining, which generally means business slows down because no one can eat outside. And that also means I can finally take a break from the espresso machine. I take a seat at the counter, turn to face the windows, and watch the rain drops ricochet off the four patio tables. Within minutes, my mind starts to wander as I try to recall the details of my dream from last night.

My dreams usually start out by the seashore. Then the woman appears: She has piercing emerald eyes, like the bottom of the Caribbean, and the darkest skin I've ever seen. She is teeny—but she has an aura of strength about her. Like I can just tell she could knock someone out if she had to. She wears all white—flowing, gauzy gowns—and multicolored beads around her neck. Her heavy silver dreadlocks, wrapped on top of her head in a turban, add at least six inches to her petite frame. The vision of her is arresting, but even more so: the feeling of her around me is intense.

Also, sometimes in my dreams, and even sometimes in the wind, I can hear another female voice calling me to the ocean. I can't explain why, but I know that this voice that calls to me is someone different from the woman I see. It's more like a spirit, or a song—like how sailors pretended that mermaids were calling them out to sea (they were really manatees, my Papi tells me). But still, the idea of being called to the shore messes me up. Because even from Brooklyn, Long Beach is still, like, an hour-long train ride away on the Long Island Rail Road. And besides, that's where all the rich white people live. Coney Island is a little closer, and I can get there on the subway, but no way Mami would let me go there by myself.

Pero for as long as I can remember, I've always loved the ocean. Last year, I asked Trini, who is a budding artist/designer taking classes at the Fashion Institute of

Technology (FIT) in Manhattan, to paint my room cerulean blue. She went the extra mile and painted beautiful images of mermaids, seahorses, shells, and my favorite, a beluga whale. I'm a Pisces, sign of the fish, so natch, water is my oasis.

"Vengan, muchachas! Time to prep the patio!" Tio Fausto's orders, accentuated with loud hand claps, make me snap back into reality. Sometime during the afternoon lull, the skies have cleared up. So that means it's time for Salma, the twins, and me to go outside to wipe down the patio tables and chairs.

Just then, a yellow cab pulls up to the curb.

The driver steps out of the taxi. He goes to the back of the cab and carefully, slowly lifts a large travel trunk out. By the looks of his body motions, the trunk is quite heavy. After struggling with it for a good minute, he puts the trunk down on the sidewalk with a resounding thud.

That thud is loud enough to get the adults' attention. Abuelo gets up from his dominoes game with Jorge. Tio Fausto and Titi Julia come out to the patio. Trini walks out too, holding Mo's hand. Abuela stands in the front doorway.

Something is happening, I can feel it.

The passenger door opens. The sun suddenly emerges from behind the cloud and shines a spotlight on a petite woman stepping onto the sidewalk.

Out on the patio, there is a collective gasp, followed by a hushed silence. I try to get around Tio and Titi to get a better look at the person who has my normally loud-as-hell family so quiet.

Abuela purses her lips and crosses her arms in front of her. Abuelo is behind her and instinctively grabs her by the shoulders. Tio Fausto does the same to Titi Julia. I look around for Mami; she's inside grabbing un cafecito from behind the counter. When I see her notice the scene unfolding outside, she looks conflicted, as if she doesn't know whether to run toward this woman or run away.

But by that point, I push past my family, so I can finally get a clear look. What I see stuns me so hard I can barely move:

The woman on the sidewalk is in all white. With multicolored beads around her neck. Locs piled atop her head in a turban. Dark, silky skin. And most importantly, those piercing green eyes like the bottom of the Caribbean.

Carajo! It's the woman from my dreams!

Siete, the awesomely giant bodega cat, has come over to investigate, and he walks figure eights around the woman's ankles, purring, like he knows her already. She stoops down to give his head a couple of skritches, then takes a few steps toward the patio, as if to greet us, but Abuela blocks her path on the sidewalk. I find it amazing that anyone could be smaller than Abuela, but there's living proof. The rest of the adults walk forward to stand behind Abuela. Things are looking very lopsided. Before I can protest, Tio Fausto makes a motion for us kids to stay on the patio.

"Trini, stay with the kids!" he adds firmly.

I'm upset for two reasons: because one, I hate being left out; and because, hello? THIS IS THE WOMAN FROM MY DREAMS AND I DESERVE TO KNOW WHO SHE IS!

My Spanglish is more English than Spanish, which means I quickly get lost by all the fast talking and the hand-waving on the sidewalk. But Trini, who I'm suddenly glad is with us kids, translates the bochinche in a gossipy whisper: "It's Titi Yaya, Abuela Chacha's estranged sister from Puerto Rico. They haven't seen each other in almost twenty years!"

The queen of Los Locos—la bruja, the "witch"—has apparently come all the way from Puerto Rico to Brooklyn! But why? And for what?

"Why not?" Ini and Mini ask in unison. Twins are really on some otherness.

"Dunno. Nobody knew what the beef was about, but no one has ever been allowed to speak to her, or of her . . . at least in my lifetime," Trini answers.

The grown-ups are still talking loudly and over each other.

Salma's Spanish is better than mine, and she always loves to show it off. "Yaya says she had to flee Puerto Rico because the big hurricane washed away her house!" she translates.

By the flurry of Abuela's hand gestures, we can all tell that she is furious—Trini translates that Abuela and her sister have been on the outs for decades *and now she just shows up?!?* But on the other hand, what can Abuela do? *Turn away her homeless sister?*

After a few minutes, Mami comes up with a compromise. She says in English, "Titi Yaya can stay in the vacant apartment above the café. It's so quiet, she won't be bothering a soul . . ."

"Especialmente tiene que dejar a los niños!" Abuela wails.

Why does Yaya need to stay away from us kids? That doesn't feel fair to anyone. And obviously, I have some weird connection to this woman I've never met but has been visiting me in my dreams. Why can't I meet her? What did she do that was so terrible?

"But I'm going to lose money!" Tio Fausto laments in English. "I spent all summer fixing up that unit. Los blanquitos would pay good money for those four walls and half a kitchen!"

"Mi amor, no one wants their shower right next to the kitchen sink," says Titi Julia, pity-patting his shoulder.

"Nunca sabes. College students are desperados," Tio Fausto retorts.

But Mami nods definitively. Basta. It's settled.

Abuela turns on her heels and storms back inside the restaurant. Abuelo Chucho looks conflicted, as if he wants to go after her, but instead, he gallantly extends his arm to escort Titi Yaya to her new living quarters using the side entrance to the building. Titi Yaya has a forlorn but resolute facial expression. Tio Fausto starts lugging her trunk behind them, grunting and cursing at its heft, but then he stops in front of us to issue a proclamation.

"Oye, here's the deal: Yaya is never to talk with you, and you are never to talk with her, ¿entienden?"

"Yes, Tio," my cousins and sister chime together. I remain tight-lipped.

"Maya?" Tio Fausto must see the defiance in my face.

"Pero, she's like, family!" I blurt out because I cannot contain myself.

"These are your Abuela's wishes. Honor them," he says.

"All right, but I feel like I should know why," I grumble and put my hands on my hips defiantly.

"Ay, Maya, maybe when you're older," Tio Fausto replies. Now I know I'm being dismissed for real.

As Abuelo Chucho leads Titi Yaya to the side entrance that leads to the apartments, her emerald eyes lock with my brown ones. What is this feeling I have? I'm light-headed, like I've been here before, but everything feels brand new at the same time.

"Now, get back to making this patio ready for the dinner shift," Tio Fausto grouses, breaking my reverie. He looks at the trunk in front of him, groans loudly, and utters a few more Spanish curse words before lifting it up again.

I turn away from Yaya to do his bidding, and then *poof!* She's gone.

As we wipe down the tables and chairs outside, Mo sits in a dry chair and Trini folds napkins while continuing to dole out more bochinche. "Oye, Titi Yaya is a bruja, like a type of witch doctor who makes potions and puts spells on people and stuff. It's called santería," she warns, as if she were telling a ghost story.

"WHOAAAAAA," says Mo, wide-eyed.

We are all hanging on to every word coming out of Trini's mouth. This is beyond bochinche. This is an actual skeletons-falling-out-of-closets type thing.

"Santería?" I ask, thinking *maybe* I've heard this word before. "But is that, like, actually *bad*, though?"

"I'm not sure. I've been in one of those botanica stores before and it's a little weird. Candles everywhere. Herbs.

But it smells good. Oh, you wanna know who I've seen come out of there though?"

"Who?" all five of us ask. This is fun. We are pretending to still clean the tables and chairs, which are already dry.

"Rosario Infante."

"Of Infante Bakery?" I ask. Señora Infante supplies the café with all our baked goods, and she never disappoints.

"Is there another Rosario Infante?" Trini asks rhetorically.

I snap the dish towel on her pompis as I walk back into the café.

AFTER A SECOND four-hour shift, I should be dog-tired, but all I want to do is sneak up that staircase and find out why this little old Black woman from Puerto Rico is invading my dreams and is now living upstairs. My cousins and Salma go home to get ready for bed. Trini is cleaning the front of the house but takes breaks to draw sketches for her fashion portfolio—that is, when she's not flirting with a customer sitting at the counter. I go into the kitchen to help Mami while I hatch my plan.

I go over to the industrial dishwasher and lift the lid, steam slapping my face. I take the pans out, and hang them on the hooks to dry. Mami puts the leftover sofrito into large containers and stashes them in the refrigerator. Fausto rolls up the large rubber floor mats to take them out back and rinse them with a hose. With Tio outside and Mami's back turned, I make my move. I inch my way across the kitchen to the corner where the staircase is. If I'm quiet enough, I might just barely make it . . .

"*Maya Beatriz!*" Mami says in a curt whisper—proving that yes, she does have eyes in the back of her head.

I'd only made it to the third step, so I quickly descend. "Yes, Mami?"

"¿Qué haces?"

"Nada—nothing!" I say, as I not-so-casually slink away from the staircase and back into the kitchen.

"You know you're not supposed to go up those stairs. Ven acá."

"OK, Mami," I say, dejected. "Pero, what's the big deal?"

"That's the rule," she says, punctuating her words with a wipe across the stainless-steel butcher block like a door shutting closed.

"Pero, she's family. What did she do to be kicked to the curb like that? That seems so mean."

I really hope I get some kind of an explanation from Mami. Maybe Trini's bochinche is wrong. Maybe this is all one big misunderstanding.

"Maybe when you're older, you'll understand." She throws the dish towel over her shoulder.

Then again, maybe asking my family anything is, and always will be, totally pointless.

I stomp my foot in protest. "Here we go. It's always, 'when you're older, Maya.' When can I have a cell phone? 'When you're older.' When can I dye my hair? 'When you're older.' Why can't I hang out at the mall just with my friends? 'When you're older.' When can I drink café con leche?' 'When you're older.' Carajo, it's getting old!"

Mami sighs heavily and leans on the butcher block in exasperation. "Ay, Maya. Ten paciencia. This is a lot for all of us to digest. Let the adults figure this one out first."

Now it's my turn to sigh. No point in continuing this conversation. "OK."

"Vete, m'ija. Go home and get ready for bed. Fausto, Trini, and I will finish up."

"OK, Mami."

But I know that I can't wait until I'm "older" to get my answers. I have to find another way.

Of course, I realize that I've never actually met Titi Yaya in real life—she's been in Puerto Rico longer than I've been alive. But I also know what I see in my dreams. I feel like I know this woman—or I'm supposed to know her. From the way she looked at me, it feels like she knows me, too.

Chapter 3

No Visitors Allowed

I CAN'T FALL ASLEEP. I have too many questions about Titi Yaya. I also miss my Papi.

My father, Eddie Montenegro, is a Mexican American civil rights attorney. He is on a yearlong sabbatical (which is kind of like a vacation where you do *other* work) from his Manhattan law firm so he can represent immigrants at the border in California. My dad is political and passionate, and he has a master's degree in history *and* a law degree. Don't get him started on the oppression of people of color everywhere around the world because he will talk your ear off.

Papi loves hyping up Chicano power. His favorite quote is from Mexican civil rights hero and United Farm

Workers founder César Chávez: "Preservation of one's own culture does not require contempt or disrespect for other cultures." This tells me to be proud of who I am and have empathy for people who don't look or act like me. Definitely words to live by.

Papi is also a huge baseball fan, so he can't *not* go on and on about the winningest team in the world, the New York Yankees. (I admit he got me rooting for them too.) But he often talks about the New York Cubans, too. They're not around anymore, thanks to desegregation, but they won the Negro League World Series in 1947.

Old movies are second only to baseball for Papi. He swoons over Rita Moreno, who won the Best Supporting Actress Oscar in the original film version of *West Side Story*, or goes on about Afro-Puerto Rican actor Juano Hernández, who went from being an acrobat in the circus, to a professional boxer in the Caribbean, to starring opposite the great Black actor, Sidney Poitier in *They Call Me Mister Tibbs!*. I love it when he drops knowledge like that.

But above all else, Papi is an intellectual. He approaches everything rationally. That means he never bought into

"Los Locos" family lore. So, I think he might be a good person for me to talk to about this Titi Yaya mess. He might have a different perspective and a different answer other than "when you're older."

I call him on the landline (yes, we still have one) and bring the cordless handset into my room.

"Hello?" His baritone voice is so soothing, like one of those old soul singers he's always playing.

"Hi Papi. It's Maya."

"¿Qué pasa, mi estrellita?" He always calls me his little star. I can't help but smile every time.

"Did Mami tell you the bochinche yet?" I ask as I climb back into bed with my free hand.

"No, what did I miss?"

"Titi Yaya just rolled up out the blue! Her house washed away in a hurricane so now she lives in the apartment above the café!!" I cover my mouth afterward for fear that I am too loud.

Papi goes silent for a moment, before asking, "Is your Abuela upset?"

"Pretty much everybody is, but especially her," I say in more hushed tones.

"What did they tell you?"

"Only that we're not to go near her," I say, holding back a pout. I leave the part out about having seen her in my dreams.

Papi harrumphs. "Figures. Did they share with you the bruja business?"

"Yeah, Trini did. So . . . is it true? Is she really a witch?"

Papi sighs before answering. "Mira, your Titi Yaya practices what's called santería. But that does not make her a bruja. It simply means she follows the religion of the Ile Ife, which started in Nigeria and was handed down from your Yoruba ancestors."

"Oh wow . . . What is Yoruba?" I ask as I scootch under the covers, bouncing my pompis down the mattress. I can tell Papi is about to go into storytelling mode, which I love, so I hunker down and get comfy.

"Your Yoruba ancestors are an African ethnic group from southwest Nigeria. Back home, they worshipped the deities of the Ile Ife, but once they were kidnapped and taken to the Caribbean, they were forced to convert to Catholicism—or be killed."

"Wait. What's Ile Ife?"

"Ile Ife is the city where the Yoruba believe their civilization began, and it's said to be the location where the orishas descended to earth. The name, Ile Ife, literally means place of dispersion."

"What's an orisha?" I go from relaxing to sitting up straight. This is getting good.

"The orishas are the gods and goddesses of the old country, and there's a whole pantheon of them. Just like there's Greek and Roman mythology, but this is African."

Papi is the best storyteller—even if he does tend to go off on tangents. And here he goes . . .

"They claim Columbus discovered America, when he really got lost in the West Indies," Papi says, chuckling. "The slave trade in the New World actually began in the early 1500s, when the Spanish Crown allowed each subject to import twelve slaves. Thus began the Triangle Trade between Europe, Africa and the Caribbean islands."

"Why does that sound so familiar?" I ask.

"It's because I've only been telling you and Salma about this since you were five years old, m'ija. That's when conquistadores would stop in West Africa to forcibly remove enslaved people from their homeland and bring them to the Caribbean to work the land—and *that's* because the Spaniards had already wiped out most of the native Taino. Then they'd return to Spain with the riches looted from the islands."

"So how did the Yoruba survive?" I am riveted. I clutch my stuffed beluga whale to my chest in anticipation for what's next.

"Well, the Yoruba practiced their religion in hiding and used the Catholic saints, like the Virgin Mary and Santa Bárbara, to hide the orishas' true identities. Hence, the name santería. This ancient religion has been kept hush-hush for centuries, but has grown more popular in the past thirty years—because it has such strong ties to the Caribbean culture and heritage. That's why many people, including Titi Yaya, are trying to preserve it."

Wow. The way Papi explains things makes so much sense—even if he didn't really answer my question.

"But listen, in your family's household, you know any talk of other religions or practices other than Christianity is forbidden. Brujería, they call it. Witchcraft. Dark magic."

There is so much more I want to learn. And Papi's history lesson isn't getting to the heart of the matter.

"Papi, do you know anything about Abuela and Titi Yaya's falling out?" Against my will, I yawn from fatigue.

"Pues, nena, it sounds like you had a long day, and it's late in Brooklyn. Go to bed, m'ija."

Carajo, I say to myself. I ruined my chance to get more info. "OK, Papi." I reply, my eyes getting heavy. Does he know something and just isn't telling me? Is he hiding something too?

"Buenas noches, mi estrellita," he says.

I put the phone down on the nightstand, next to my music box.

Whenever I need to zone out or chill out, I wind up my favorite music box. It has this kind of haunting tune that I can never quite identify, almost Debussy-like (yes, Papi makes us listen to classical music too), yet it somehow always manages to calm me down. Plus, I just love to stare at it.

The music box is made of carved cherrywood and has all sorts of tiny details, including a mother of pearl border around it that looks like little waves on the sides. The lid has a mini statuette of a mermaid and fish, plus real conch shells, and bits of coral embedded in it. It's a bit mangled on the outside, but it is a gift handed down to me from my favorite aunt, Titi Dolores. I have to say this is my most prized possession.

As the tune plays, I think more about Titi Yaya. She doesn't seem like the bruja my family (other than Papi) made her out to be. Like, the kind of witch who goes around casting evil spells on folks and stuff? Or like a voodoo witch doctor who makes live animal sacrifices and pours blood all over themselves? I find either of these scenarios hard to believe. Her face looks too kind.

Then I think about those botanicas in the neighborhood that Trini mentioned earlier, whose windows are filled with statues of saints, powders, candles, and beads, and drum music to lure you in. While I was always curious to go in, Mami told me to walk past them. Maybe I should've paid more attention to what those stores were hawking? I make a mental note to check one out one day.

Actually, I am not much of a believer in anything. I am like my Papi in that way—always rational and super curious. And like him, I need to see the evidence—read it, examine it, hold it in my hot little hands—to become a believer.

Mami, on the other hand, is super religious. She carries her rosary beads wherever she goes. I can always hear her whispering makeshift prayers under her breath whenever we kids do something she doesn't like. The woman doesn't even like too many candles lit in the house at once, thinking they will summon evil spirits or something like that. I swear, sometimes the most religious people are the most superstitious. Papi is agnostic, which means he believes that something like a higher being is unknowable, and therefore questions the existence of God. He tells Salma and me to not make fun of Mami's rituals, no matter how strange or nonsensical they seem. But if Mami is so God-fearing, why did she insist that Titi Yaya stay?

Sense or no sense, faith or no faith, this "no visitors allowed" routine with Titi Yaya is wack—and a rule that is just itching to be broken. After all, it isn't very Christian-like to ban your own family member. My family is usually so loving to one another, it just doesn't make sense that they could hate on another relative so ferociously.

As I drift off to sleep, I wonder: What happened that was so bad it would cause a twenty-year rift between sisters? And yo, what does this have to do with me all of the sudden?

Chapter 4

The Last Day of Summer

Labor Day. One of the only four days the café closes during the year. It's an annual tradition for the Calderones-Montenegros to head to the beach. And, unbeknownst to anyone else, maybe I can finally figure out why the ocean has been calling me.

Per the usual holiday routine, that morning at the crack of dawn, we pack a cooler full of ham and cheese sandwiches, chips, canned soda, and bottled water; grab an umbrella, blankets, and beach chairs; and haul it all on the R train to make the forty-five-minute ride to Coney Island.

While Mami is in the kitchen making the sandwiches, I am trying to get my act together. I am in the foyer putting my flip flops on when I call out:

"Mami, can I bring my soccer ball?"

"Yes, just remember: You bring it, you're responsible for it," she calls back.

I walk into the kitchen and then ask a question I know the answer to, just to suss out Mami's reaction. "So, is Titi Yaya coming with us?"

I am shut down with "that look." Every Latina mom has it. The one that says, "Don't cross me."

WE AREN'T THE ONLY family from the neighborhood going to hang out in Coney Island. The train is packed with other groups of brown people toting all their beach gear to the nearest piece of ocean in the city. The blanquito gentrifiers tend to take the LIRR to the fancy beaches there, and the really rich ones head to the Hamptons, but Coney Island is much more for us regular people. Plus, it has the Wonder Wheel, the giant Ferris wheel that offers awesome views of the whole city.

Once we arrive at the shore, it takes forever for us to find the right spot on the beach.

"We need to be able to make a quick getaway in case

it gets too crowded," Tio Fausto says. The only crowds he likes are when the restaurant is full.

"We want to be near the arcade," the twins whine in unison.

"I want to be close to the water!" Mo exclaims.

Mami quietly negotiates a place for us—not too far from the arcade, and not too far from the water. "We camp here," she says. The Queen of the Compromise wins again.

After we settle into our patch of sand with a big blanket, a couple of beach chairs, and an umbrella, our parents give us some money for the arcade and the Wonder Wheel. Primo Mo stays behind to start his creation with a bucket and shovel.

I decide to take some of my arcade money to buy a Mexican mango (served on a stick and cut to look like a flower, doused in lime juice, salt, and picante sauce). As soon as I make my purchase from the fruit cart, I see Kayla Phillips, my friend and teammate on my soccer team in the distance. She is fly as all get-out—with a glorious afro, almond-shaped eyes, a heart-shaped mouth, and body built like a track star. She spots me because we both have our soccer jerseys on over our bathing suits. We've known each other since sixth grade, but lately, she makes me feel goofy whenever she is nearby. But with fourteen goals between us, we are a force to be reckoned with on the soccer pitch. Of course, she comes up to me at the exact same moment when I have a mouth full of mango.

"Hi, Maya!" Kayla says enthusiastically.

Mango juice drips down my chin. I have no napkins, so I use the back of my hand to wipe my face and try to hide my embarrassment. "Um . . . Hi, Kayla."

It didn't used to be like this with Kayla. Usually, a little sloppiness between teammates is nothing. But lately . . . I don't know. Something is different, and I don't want her to see me as goofy, sloppy Maya. I want her to see me as . . . something else.

"I've never had one of those. Are they any good?"

"Ohmigosh, they're only the best thing ever!" I squeal, forgetting to be cool and immediately slipping back into our normal, old rhythm.

"OK, I'll try it. Why not?" She turns to order a mango on a stick for herself. She takes the plastic sandwich bag, holds it upright, and asks, "Like this?" And then she starts marinating the concoction over the mango.

"Yup. Perfecta."

"Ok, now what?" she asks.

"Well, you take off the plastic bag. I like starting from the bottom, where most of the meat is. Either way, it's pretty messy," I say, although I bet Kayla can make even this look elegant.

"Ohhhhh, it's sooooo good!" Kayla exclaims, before diving in for another bite. Now she has mango juice dripping down her chin too. We both start laughing. I go back to the cart to ask for servilletas, and I hand her a few.

"Mayaaaaa!" Salma calls behind me.

"What, Sal?" I call back, only slightly annoyed that my moment with Kayla is being interrupted.

"We're going on the Wonder Wheel!" she exclaims.

"Come on!" Ini and Mini add in unison.

I don't want this moment to end. But before I can say anything, Kayla says,

"Well, do you have room for a plus-one?"

Well, this is an interesting development.

"Yeah, sure," I say happily. "I'll introduce you to my wacky family."

We catch up to Salma and the twins. "Kayla, this is my little sister Salma, and my twin cousins Ini and Mini."

Everybody says hi at once.

"What's up, y'all?" Kayla says.

"Where's Trini?" I ask.

"She's over there flirting with the ticket salesman," Salma answers, rolling her eyes.

"Yeah, but we get to ride . . ." starts Ini.

"For FREE!" finishes Mini.

"Let's find her and get in line," I say.

Sure enough, Trini is right where the girls left her, by the ticket counter. She is leaning her head on her hand, pretending to hang on dude's every word.

"Trini, we're ready!" Salma says.

"Oh, there are my nieces," Trini says, trying to sound older.

"Trini, I brought a friend. Can we get a ticket for her too?" I ask.

"Not a problem," says the ticket salesman. He hands us each a blue ticket. "Here you go, girls. Enjoy the wonder of the Wonder Wheel!" he adds with a wink. Ugh. So corny. He probably says that a hundred and forty-seven times a day.

We each mutter a thank-you and head to the line. Kayla and I have finished our mangoes, but as we both note when we high-five, our hands are still sticky.

As the line inches forward (I count eleven people ahead of us, impatient as I am to fly over Coney Island and sitting next to Kayla), I hear a male voice yell my name.

"Hey, Maya!"

I turn around, and my heart sinks. It's Nestor Garcia. I hadn't seen him all summer (and I was glad for that). From the very first day of middle school two years ago, he has proclaimed his love for me to anyone who would listen—and he hasn't stopped.

I notice Nestor grew at least like half a foot over the summer and now has a faint mustache. It's not that he isn't a good guy and, although he's gangly now, he isn't bad looking. I'm just not into him. And you don't want to hear daily professions of love from a guy who you just consider mid. As a matter of fact, I'm not sure if I'm even into boys at all. I still feel the mango residue from Kayla's high five sticking to my fingers and that makes me smile, but I can't let Nestor think it's for him.

"Hi, Nestor," I say, trying not to feel too guilty about how glum I sound.

"I didn't know you'd be here!" he says, leaning in a little too close.

As if.

"Dude, we come here every year," I reply as I take what I hope is a subtle step back, careful not to bump into the people in front of us. I do not need this boy's dragon breath in my face right now.

"Oh, right. Riding the Wonder Wheel, huh?"

Get a grip, man! "Yeah, uh, that's why we're in line." I gesture to Kayla and my cousins. I am so ready for someone else—*any*one else—to enter this conversation.

"Oh. Yeah. Heh. Hey Kayla, how are you?" Nestor says it like he's just noticing we aren't alone. He really is clueless.

"Fine, thanks." Kayla nods and goes back to her phone.

"You guys ready for school tomorrow?" he asks.

"I'd rather not think about it while I'm at the beach," I say matter-of-factly.

"Oh, uh, yeah, you're right." Nestor lets out a nervous laugh and his face turns red. "Anyway, OK . . . enjoy your last day of summer! I'll, uh, see you at school."

"OK, later." I finish. I turn to Kayla, who is still scrolling her phone, obviously having already checked out of the conversation.

When Nestor is a safe distance away, Kayla looks up from her phone and says to me, "Well, *that* was awkward."

"Yeah, I know. He's a nice guy. I just wish he would get the hint."

"Eh. Can't blame someone for shooting their shot," she says with a wry smile. Is that supposed to mean something else?

When we finally reach the front of the line, all six of us scurry into one of the cars and the attendant locks the door. In a few minutes, we take off with a herky-jerky motion and are slowly propelled into the air. Midway through, the ride gives each car a chance to stop at the top for a couple minutes to take in the view—from the shoreline to the Brooklyn skyline. This is my favorite part.

I look over to see if Kayla is equally impressed. She is. I smile.

"Trini, can you take some pictures with your phone?" I ask.

"Sure. Y'all get on one side," Trini says.

Salma, Ini, and Mini get on Kayla's and my side of the car, and we all cheese for the camera.

After the twins go back to their side, Kayla breaks out her phone.

"Selfie time!" she says as she puts a still-sticky hand on my shoulder and pulls me toward her. This one is just of me and her. She looks at the image of us on her phone and adds, "We cute." She shows me and I have to agree. My heart flips seeing us together like that.

When we get off the ride, Kayla texts her mom to make sure it's cool to continue hanging out with us. We head back to the beach, where Mami and Titi Julia are chilling under the umbrella—chatting instead of paying attention to their paperback romance novels. Trini goes to lay in the sun in her bikini, to get a tan. Tio Fausto is helping Mo build his sand masterpiece, which is many castles surrounded by a serpentine moat.

"¿Tienen hambre, muchachas?" Of course, Latina moms always ask if you're hungry, especially on a day at the beach. "Oh, hi Kayla," Mami says.

"Hello, Mrs. Montenegro," Kayla says.

"You're welcome to a sandwich," Titi Julia chimes in.

"Oh, I'm good," Kayla says, eyeing the overflowing cooler in the sand.

"How 'bout we split one?" I suggest. I can tell she is just being polite, and there is no way I am letting my friend go hungry while spending the day with me. That's just not the Calderon way!

"Oh OK. Sure," she replies gratefully.

My cousins, sister, Kayla, and I gather around the cooler to collect our ham-filled blessings. The sandwiches are on Infante Bakery's French bread, which has all that doughy goodness with the crunch on top. I plop down on another blanket opposite Trini that's also in the sun, and sit down. Kayla follows suit. I hand her half of my sandwich. She takes a bite and gives out a slight moan.

"Dang, Maya, your family makes the best food." She takes another hearty bite and talks before she can swallow.

"I'm gonna make my mom take me to Café Taza again soon. It's been too long."

"Aight, cool," I say. I hide a slight grin behind my soda can. "You right, it has been a minute. Maybe you can come one evening after soccer practice or something."

"Yeah, maybe. We'll figure it out." Kayla quickly wolfs down her half of the ham sandwich. "But speaking of practice, you want to go kick the ball around when you're done?" she asks.

"Sure, I need to practice before the game next weekend."

Part of me wants to get up right away, but it feels so good sitting next to Kayla and squishing my toes in the sand. I decide to savor my last few bites.

"Why? Everyone knows you're the star," says Kayla. She playfully pushes my shoulder.

I blush for a hot second. "Naw, girl, it's *you*," I reply. I shove her back.

"Well, we do kind of make a great team." Is she blushing now?

"Truuuuuueeeee," I say. And we clink soda cans.

Does this mean we're a good team on or off the soccer pitch? Or is it both? I squish my toes in the sand again and wonder to myself.

After Mami insists I put another layer of sunscreen on, Kayla and I walk to an open stretch of sand by the shoreline, free from any viejitos on their beach chairs, or kids with their pails and shovels. I jog about thirty feet away from her and drop-bounce-kick the soccer ball over. She stops the ball with her right foot, centers it, then kicks it in the air to me. I stop the ball with my chest, where it dribbles down to my feet. I square up and kick it with my left foot back to her. We keep moving the ball to simulate us passing it back and forth on the pitch.

On our U13 team, the Warriors, I'm the CAM: center attacking midfielder. Kayla plays halfback. I'm offense and she's a hybrid of offense and defense. Whenever we're in sync, we usually win. Coach says both of us could have a big future if we want it bad enough—college scholarships and everything. I've heard random adults say this could be our ticket out of el barrio.

All the sudden, a sturdy girl wearing board shorts and a swim T-shirt intercepts the ball and dribbles away with it.

Carajo, it's Gina Sardino.

Gina is the goalie of our biggest rivals, the Honey Badgers. Offense vs. Defense. The classic duel. We play them next weekend.

Gina has beef with me because of all the goals I've scored on her. She is the most brutish of bullies on an already dirty squad—checking in at about five foot ten and built of solid muscle, which is about three inches and several pounds more than me. I'm pretty average, but with bigger thighs and feet, which is probably why I'm good at soccer.

Gina cackles, "Ahahahahahaha, y'all so weak with it. Look how easy it was for me to steal the ball."

"We weren't playing for real, Gina. Now give it back!" I call.

"Nah, I think I'll keep it for a little while," and she dribbles it up shore till she hits the sand. Kayla and I chase after her until she picks up the soccer ball and drop-kicks it right into Mo's sandcastle empire. Mo stands up and looks around to see where the ball came from and then bursts out crying. Tio Fausto witnesses what happened and stares directly at Gina, who suddenly looks sheepish.

Gina turns to go, but not before she points at me and mimes choking herself, like that's what I'm going to do on Saturday. I think about running after her, but instead I jog over to my baby cousin to console him.

"We can rebuild it," I tell Mo.

"Oh-oh-OK," he hiccups, wiping his sandy hands over his tear-stained eyes.

Just then, Kayla's phone buzzes.

"It's my mom. She says we're leaving. I—I gotta go. I'm so sorry I can't stay and help."

"No need to apologize. I had a great time," I say, trying to hide my disappointment.

"Me too. Uh, see you tomorrow at school."

Kayla goes to give me a hug. I may be awkwardly lingering a few extra seconds, but she doesn't seem to mind.

"OK," I say. "Bye for now."

After I watch Kayla leave, I turn to help Mo rebuild his sandcastle. But my friend stays on my mind. A few minutes later, however, I see the tide starting to come in. And in a second, my original urge to head into the water hits me like a massive wave.

"Does anyone want to join me in the ocean?" I ask no one in particular.

"If you do, hurry up, because we're getting ready to go," Mami cautions.

"I won't be long, I promise. I just want to take a dip," I assure her.

I take off my soccer jersey, adjust my tankini, and jog to the shoreline. As soon as the water laps at my feet, I hear a female voice in the wind, like someone calling to me. The further I wade into the water, the stronger this female voice becomes:

"Ven a mí." *Come to me*, the voice says.

OK . . . this is just how my dreams start. Only now, I'm not dreaming. I'm slightly freaked out, but I take a few tentative steps forward.

"Ven a mí," the breeze calls again.

The waves are now hitting my calves. I continue to go further into the ocean, until I am thigh deep.

"Ven a mí," the winds whisper again.

As if in a trance, I wade in the ocean chest-deep. I wonder if I can hear the voice if I go underwater. I dive through a wave.

"Ven a mí," she says once more. The mellifluous voice is muffled but still clear.

I can feel a rip current pulling me in more. I dive through another wave to see if I can escape it. But the current keeps getting stronger and taking me farther and farther away from the shore. I try to paddle back in, to no avail. But just as I start to panic, I feel two arms wrap around me.

When I pop back up, I am sputtering, but I swear I see a figure fading in the distance. I try to focus but am interrupted by the lifeguard holding me.

"The rip current is too strong for you to be out here, missy," she says as she pulls me ashore with the help of her buoy.

Mi familia is all watching terrified while I am being rescued. I put my hands on my knees and take in all the oxygen I can. Mami comes running to hold me.

"¿Qué estabas pensando, m'ija? Didn't you see the flag for the rip tide?"

"No, Mami."

"¿Estás OK?" She stops to grab a beach towel and wraps it around me. I hug myself with it. She holds my face in her hands and peers into my eyes.

"Sí, Mami. I'm fine." But my teeth are slightly chattering.

"You scared me half to death!" she exclaims.

"I know. I'm sorry, Mami." I look down, suddenly embarrassed.

"Let's get you home."

"OK, Mami." And I let her lead me back to the sandy spot where our stuff used to be.

ON THE WAY BACK on the subway, I think about how this day was so wonderful and so weird at the same time—from hearing Kayla's laugh on the Wonder Wheel, to a mysterious siren song in the ocean, to me almost drowning.

As we're heading home, Salma sidles up to me on the plastic orange and yellow bench and asks, "Hey, are you OK?"

I pause as I try to gather my thoughts. I am still freaked out by what happened at the beach. I'm normally a good swimmer, so why did I lose control like that? Instead, I just say, "Yeah, I'm good," and offer her a slight grin.

"Good, cuz that was a pretty stupid stunt you pulled," she scoffs. Of course, my lil' sis can't just be concerned; she has to get a dig in.

"Thanks, hermana." I decide to let her have this one. I also decide midway through the train ride home that I need to see Titi Yaya tonight, no matter what. I have to get to the bottom of this mystery.

Chapter 5

Dark Electric Night

IT'S NOT EASY sneaking out of the house—not impossible, however, for athletically inclined folk like myself.

My room and Salma's room are on the second floor of our brownstone. My parents' room is on the third floor. Los abuelos live in the basement apartment. I wait till I know Mami falls asleep (which is usually about fifteen minutes after the monologue on *The Late Show*), and tiptoe downstairs into the hallway and quietly grab her keys. I can't risk just walking out the front door. So, I go back upstairs, close the door to my room, and change into some navy-blue leggings, a matching hoodie, and my lighter-than-air sneakers. I crack open the window and creep out onto the fire escape. I place a stick in the crack of the windowsill—that way, I don't lock myself out of the house accidentally and really get myself into trouble.

Lucky for me, the café is only a block and a half from the house. Though I gotta admit, it's kinda creepy to be out on the streets of Brooklyn after midnight. I feel like running down the block on Fulton Street at top speed, but I know that will only draw attention and suspicion if any cops are around—and they usually are. That's one thing about gentrification: while crime usually goes down, which I guess is good, los blanquitos are always calling the police for every little thing. Still, Papi taught me decent urban survival skills: if I walk fast, alert, and with purpose, nobody—cops, bums, whoever—will really bother me. Wait a minute . . . I spot a new storefront on the block. Is that a restaurant that just sells . . . broccoli? I shake my head and roll my eyes. I can't wait to tell Abuelo about that one.

I breathe a sigh of relief when I make it to the scratched blue front door of Café Taza. But then Siete's loud meow causes me to jump out of my skin.

"Siete! What are you doing here?" I whisper yell. The chonky cat answers with two more meows. He could very well be asking me the same thing. Seems we both are sneaking out. Only the stakes are much higher for me. Siete can't get grounded.

Siete's loud purrs calm me down a bit before I decide to commit my crime and break in. (Though is it breaking and entering if I have the key?) I take a deep breath and quietly unlock the door, walk through the empty dining room, into the kitchen, and stop at the back steps that lead to where the apartments are.

I stand at the foot of the stairs and stare upward for a long hard minute. The door at the top of the stairs is cracked open slightly, with a glow emanating from it. The thumping of my heart seems loud enough to be heard all the way to Prospect Park, and I freeze for a second waiting for Mami to hear it and come snatch me by the ear any minute. When I realize no one is there to bust me, I tiptoe up the staircase as quietly as my Nikes allow.

As I near the top of the stairs, I can hear a familiar voice behind the door, and I gasp. It's Abuela Chacha! What is she doing here?

I overhear muttering in a combination of Spanish, English, and a language I've never heard before. I stand as close to the doorframe as possible to listen without being spotted. If I'm caught, I'll pay a hefty price, like having to wash the dishes at the café for a week. And I'd definitely lose internet privileges. Luckily, I can see through the crack that Abuela has her back to the door, so she can't see me. But she sounds agitated.

"Cuánto tiempo estarás aquí?" She's demanding to know how long Titi Yaya will be staying here, and from the sound of her voice, it's clear that Titi Yaya can't leave fast enough for her liking.

Titi Yaya responds in a calm, husky voice. "No sé, Chavela. No tengo nada en Puerto Rico ahora. I lose everything."

I've never heard anyone call Abuela by her birth name before. Abuela looks humbled by it. I guess big sisters have a way of putting their younger siblings in check. I should know.

"And what will happen now with you here?" Abuela says.

"Iwa e lo'n ba l'eru," Yaya says.

I don't recognize that language. By the look on Abuela's face, neither does she.

"Your Lucumí is rusty," Titi Yaya says with a low chuckle. "It is your past behavior that scares you. Not mine," she translates.

Through the crack of the door, I watch Yaya take something out of her trunk. She pulls out a bulky object covered in a velvet cloth, and it seems like it would be heavy. But she manages to set it down on the floor with ease and remove the tapestry that covers it. Underneath is a cast-iron cauldron that probably weighs more than she does.

Then, she goes back to the trunk, where she pulls out a series of mason jars, one by one, each larger than the next, with different powder-like substances and dried-up herbs, leaves, and flowers in the containers.

She removes a couple of güiros—hollowed-out, dried-out gourds with ridges on them. I recognize them from salsa music; güiros are used as a percussion instrument (you play them with something that looks like a metal afro pick). But these seem to have stuff inside them, cuz she opens one up by the seam and sniffs the contents inside.

"Sí, está maduro," she says to no one in particular. Meaning that whatever she has in there, it's ripe.

Abuela breaks her silence. "Bueno, you're here now. I'm not going to kick you out. It would break Soledad's heart," she adds. What does Mami have to do with this?

Then, Abuela gives a firm directive: "Pero oye, I don't want any of your brujería near the children, ¿entiendes?"

"As you wish, mi hermana. Pero, each spirit has her own free will."

Is she talking about me? At that moment, ever so briefly, Titi Yaya turns her face to me. I freeze mid-squat as her emerald eyes flash once again, making direct contact with my baby browns, locking for a nanosecond. There is just a hint of a smile behind them. Stunned by her ethereal beauty, I can't help but grin back at her.

Then, a second flash of brilliance hits my eyes: a shiny ebony stone she is wearing around her neck, among the turquoise and other colored beads that remind me of the waters off the island itself. She puts her hand over it and touches it. Immediately, I feel a rush of energy pass through me, like one of those static electricity shocks you get after walking too quickly on carpet.

I gasp from the sensation, then quickly cover my mouth. This is becoming too intense for me to handle. Plus, I am afraid I will be busted by Abuela soon if I let out one more peep. She might totally lose it if she sees that I've so blatantly disobeyed her. So I hightail it back down the stairs as quietly as I can, before anyone can catch wind.

Once outside, I run full blast back up the block and to our building—this time without caring about cops, bums, whoever can try and stop me.

I climb up the fire escape, crawl through the window, put my trusty stick back in its hiding place, kick off my kicks, and tiptoe downstairs to return Mami's keys. Then, I scramble back into my bed before I can wake up Salma next door.

I have so many weird and intense feelings. Why is Abuela so intent on keeping us kids away from her sister? Why does it feel like my connection to Titi Yaya seems to get stronger every time I see her? My adrenaline is pumping. I start to hyperventilate. Chills are shivering down my spine. I obviously can't go to anyone about this sudden condition. I take a swig of water from the bottle on my nightstand. The only thing I can think of is to pick up my music box again, turn the key, and listen to its hypnotic tune over and over again until my teeth stop chattering and my heart stops racing.

As the music box works its magic, I feel my eyelids grow heavier and my breath slow down. I drift into a different state of slumber. But before seeing the blackness that sleep usually brings, I see a flash of white . . .

Chapter 6

Sea Dreams

I FIND MYSELF on a beach of pure white sand. It is night. I am walking along the shore, following the moonbeams, listening to the tide roll in. I am wearing a white tee, and a long white gauze skirt, with seven sheer petticoats underneath, in all the magnificent green and blue tones of the Caribbean Sea. The layers of my skirt swish and blow in the wind, mirroring the rhythm of the tides, while the mist of the ocean hits my face. I am at peace.

The full moon focuses its brightest beam on a shiny object off in the distance. The shaft of light compels me to walk toward the source of the reflecting light. When I reach it, I kneel down, and see that it is a stone—slick, shiny, and blacker than the night itself. Just then, a female voice emerges from the sea, carried by the crosswinds, which swirl all around me.

"Soy Yemaya Olokun. Tómalo," the voice tells me.

So, the voice has a name. But what does it mean? Nevertheless, I do just as she commands and pick up the stone. I rub it in between my hands, thinking it'll call forth the owner of the voice like a genie. I look around, but no one appears. I turn toward the ocean and take a few timid steps into the water.

"Who are you? Where are you?" I call out. I begin to venture out a little further into the ocean. I think that perhaps the voice is behind the waves somewhere.

"Póntelo, m'ija."

"What for?" I ask. I wade further into the sea, trying to look for the figure calling me from beyond the waves.

"To protect you."

The ocean hisses while waves break with their force against my thighs.

"But why? Who are you?"

I am practically swimming against the burgeoning current in the foamy water, now waist-deep, desperate to find an answer, a clue, anything.

"What am I looking for?" I ask.

"Busca tu aché," the voice says.

"My what?"

"Do not be afraid of what you do not know," the wind echoes around me in both Spanish and English.

Then a gigantic tidal wave crashes over me.

My eyes open abruptly and I am gasping for air, drowning in the sea of my blue sheets and lilac blankets. My heart is racing once again. Forehead wet with perspiration. The sun is just coming up. I untangle myself from the covers and in the process, I hear a hard object hit the floor and make a distinctive *clack*.

I catapult off the mattress, landing on all fours on the floor, and come face to face with it.

The black stone from my dream.

I brought it back with me.

I stare at the stone—a smaller version of what I saw, about the size of a gold Sacagawea dollar coin with a small hole near its rim. It is shinier than ebony, so smooth—so glossy that I can see my reflection in it. I rub my eyes, not quite believing what I am seeing. Is this the same black stone that Titi Yaya was wearing around her neck last night? The stone feels cool and slightly damp, as if it were just plucked fresh from the ocean itself. As I caress its smooth surface, I look around my room to see if anything else had been disturbed while I was asleep.

Nope, everything is in its usual state of disarray. The window is still slightly open, just as I left it when I crept back in. Stuffed animals are still propped up against my crowded bookcase in the corner of my room. About a half dozen pairs of kicks are spilling out of my closet. Everything is in its haphazard place.

The rock burns in my hand like an ice cube.

Chapter 7

Leche con Café

SOMEHOW IN MY stupefied state, I still manage to put myself together for the first day of school. (I may be groggy, but I still gotta look cute!) Wearing the same navy leggings from last night, I put on a plaid flannel over a graphic T-shirt. As I fix my hair, I keep glancing over at the stone, which I feel like is staring back at me from my nightstand. I can't make any sense out of how a stone went from Titi Yaya's neck, to my dream, and into my bed. Still, I don't want to leave it just lying around for Mami, or a snooping Salma, to find. I stuff it in my messenger bag and bound downstairs for some breakfast, trying to mentally prepare myself to live a regular day as a new eighth grader, as if my world hasn't just been rocked.

I plop down at the kitchen table and Mami places a hot bowl of oatmeal in front of me.

"Did you remember to pack your cleats, Maya?" Mami asks me.

"Carajo! I forgot today was practice!"

"Finish your avena, m'ija. I'll get them. Can't let the star midfielder forget her equipment now, can we?" Mami can never hide the pride in her voice and musses up my hair before walking away.

As soon Mami is out of earshot, Salma begins clowning me. "'Can't let the star midfielder forget her equipment now, can we?'" she repeats like a whiny parrot.

"Ay, Salchicha! Get over it!" I say, scrunching up my curly 'do as my still damp hair dries. I am in no mood to battle and I know calling her a sausage will shut her up.

See, in the spirit of big sisters everywhere, I must anoint my hermanita with a cruel nickname. Latines affectionately refer to Salma as "bien gordita," because being full-figured is admired in the Latine community. Everything about her is plump: her little soft panzita, big, bee-stung lips, corkscrew rizos that frame her heart-shaped face with manzanita cheeks, and bright round eyes with thick eyelashes that can't even be hidden behind her tortoise-shell glasses. On the low, she's actually quite stunning. But I'll never let her know that. To Salchicha, I'm the all-knowing, ever beautiful trigueña Mayan maiden princess, and she is the prickly pear cactus who stands forever in my shadow.

"OK, girls!" Mami calls from the top of the stairs. "Es la hora! Time to go!"

Mami stuffs a tote bag with my cleats, shin guards, kneepads, and socks and places it next to my messenger bag. "Toma. Y váyanse. Get out of here before you're late."

She is practically shoving us out the door. "Pick up your primos and head straight to school, OK?"

"Sí, Mami," we chant.

"And don't stop by the panadería either!" she commands as she ushers us out the door.

"No, Mami."

"Señora Infante is not obligated to give you a second breakfast, ¿entienden?" she calls from the front of the stoop.

"Sí, Mami."

And half-muttering to herself, she says, "She must think I'm the worst mother in the world, that I don't feed my children breakfast."

"Sí, Mami."

But by the time we walk around the corner and down the two blocks to fetch Ini, Mini, and Mo on St. James Street, our empty promise is long forgotten. Every Monday through Friday, we hear that same speech, and every Monday through Friday, we manage to ignore it. Four more blocks later, all five of us find ourselves at the Infante Bakery counter just as it opens.

Señora Rosario Infante is a large, sweet woman who obviously enjoys the fruits of her baked labor. Her bread, galletas, and dulces are simply the best. Tío Fausto says her baked goods help make our restaurant even better.

Expecting us, she's already prepared our pan tostado, doused with butter and jam, which always makes us feel like we'd died and gone to heaven. Each of us offer up our muffled, mandatory "gracias" after our first bite, butter dripping down our greedy chins.

But after last night, I need something more than oatmeal and bread. Maybe a shot of caffeine can zap me back to my senses.

"Señora, could I trouble you for a café con mucho, mucho leche?" I ask as sweetly as I can, breaking through to the front of the pack.

Señora Infante chuckles with her whole body. "Now, you know your family's restaurant has the best cafés in Brooklyn, Maya. Why do you ask me for my muddy brown water?"

"Mami says I'm too young to form the habit," I say, feeling the familiar indignation well up in me as I admit the truth.

Why is it always the same thing with Mami? I suppose she'd also say I'm too young to go catching stones from dreams, and yet that thing might be burning a hole in my messenger bag right now for all I know. What would she say then?

"Why would I want to go against your mami's wishes?" she asks in a lilting, teasing tone.

"¿Por favor, Señora?"

Señora Infante chuckles again at my answer. I can sense a yes coming. So, I milk it with the puppy dog eyes. "Please? I'll even pay for it!"

"Maaay-yaaa," Salma says from over by the door. "We're gonna be late for school!"

"Chill, Sal!" I say, waving over my shoulder at her to go on without me.

"Now, now. This will only take a momentito," Señora Infante laughs, as she makes her way to the coffeemaker.

Salma adjusts her glasses to give me el mal ojo. "Come on, girls . . ." she mutters to Ini and Mini.

"Heeeeey!" Mo protests.

"Sorry, Mo. And *guy* . . . Let's wait for Señorita Bustelo outside." Salma huffs and spins around. She throws the door open, making that bell jingle furiously.

I prop my bag on the counter and start digging for loose change. Señora Infante hands me a steaming to-go cup.

"Now, now, Maya Calderon Montenegro. You know your money's no good here." She holds a hand up to stop me like a crossing guard.

"No, no, Señora, I insist," I say. She feeds us second breakfast every day, after all. It's the least I could do.

I think I feel a couple of quarters at the bottom of my bag. But by jerking my hand up, the mystery stone from my dream pops out of my bag and lands smack dab on the counter. The señora and I both stop cold and stare at it for a long minute as it makes that sound like a spinning top, losing its spin.

"Maya, dear, why on earth would you have an azabache?" she asks.

"A what?" I give her a confused look.

"An azabache. That stone right there. Where did you get it?"

Shoot. Busted. "Uh, um, uh, I don't know . . . I found it?" It sounds like more of a question than an answer.

"No, no, no," she says, tut-tutting while shaking her head. "You cannot just find such things. Someone had to have given it to you. Someone special."

I blow the steam off the top of my milky coffee drink and take a cautious sip while I try to think of an answer that won't make Señora Infante call my parents—or the loony bin for that matter—but instead a question finds its way out of my mouth.

"So, uh, why would someone want to give this thing—this ah-zah-bah-che—to someone anyway?" I ask, trying my bestest to sound all casual.

"It wards off evil spirits," the Señora answers. "Someone must want to protect you."

Ohmigosh! The voice from my dream! That's exactly what it said! I drop my paper cup and hot liquid spills everywhere.

"Ay! Señora Infante! Lo siento . . . I'm not usually such a klutz!"

I try to reach for the napkin dispenser on top of the display counter, but end up knocking the whole tin over, which sends napkins scattering everywhere.

"Ohmigosh, I'm soooo sorry! . . ." I say. Totally flustered, I am now pacing in little circles.

"No, m'ija, don't worry. I'll clean up. Just go to school. Vete!" she says, shooing me away with her hands, but her eyes show concern.

I grab my bag with my right hand and scoop the stone with my left, then head out. Señora Infante squats down to wipe up my mess. Under her labored breathing, I swear I hear her say, "Y cuídate."

As I push the door open with my right hand, I unclench my left fist and stare at the stone again.

Careful? What do I have to be careful of? This is the second time in the past twelve hours that I've been told I need protection—first, the voice in my dream, and now, Señora Infante. Protection from what? Or whom? And why?

ALL MORNING, my curiosity gets the best of me and I can barely concentrate during my classes. So, on my lunch break, I decide to go to the school library to do some research. I tell the librarian I'm getting a head start on my science project and walk over to the computer lab, where I open up one of the Chromebooks that are there for students. A quick Google search tells me that an azabache is a black stone (duh) that, according to Puerto Rican folklore, is meant to ward off evil spirits. It's usually given to babies to wear around their neck or wrist to protect them against el mal ojo or from any jealousy. (Carajo, I should've had this years ago! I get both several times a day from Salma!) But adults can wear them too. But besides my sister, who else is jealous of me?

Gina Sardino, that's who. She always swears up and down when she passes me in the hallways that she'll get me one of these days. And get me good. Based on her bully-ball episode at the beach last weekend, I have a feeling she'll try to live up to that threat on Saturday. That's when the Warriors will face off against the Honey Badgers. So, yeah, I better figure out how to wear this thing this week—and not get busted doing it.

When I get home from school, I go upstairs to my room and open my jewelry box that is on the dresser. After scrounging around, I find a leather cord left over from my jewelry-crafting phase that is thin enough to go through the small hole in the stone. I pull it through and tie it around my neck—tight enough so that it won't fall off, but loose enough that I can hide it under my T-shirt. No V-necks for me this week!

Wearing the azabache suddenly gives me a sense of calm I never knew I needed.

Chapter 8

Offense vs. Defense

MATCH DAYS MEANS that Tio Fausto gives me a break from working the brunch shift—to Salma's chagrin, of course. Yo, I can't help it that I'm a soccer star!

I guess Tio is feeling generous today, because he also lets Ini and Mini come with me—and the twins are psyched. The one thing that I can count on my twin cousins being good for is a pretty decent cheerleading section, even if they are a little pitchy. Salma isn't into sports—she is more of a homebody who would rather sleep in than swim, or watch movies rather than move unnecessarily— so she volunteers to stay at the café to look after Mo.

I kind of wish my hermanita would be more support-ive of me. But one thing I know for sure: Salma hates—I mean, haaaaaates—watching me excel in my element. Probably because she's still searching for something to be good at herself. She just started taking guitar lessons and she's not horrible at it. Also, she loves to help Mami in the kitchen—so who knows? Maybe she'll take over the restaurant one day. But yo, I don't have time to dwell on my sister's future right now. I have a game to think about winning.

By the time I arrive on the pitch, Gina is bumping into my teammates as they bend down to tie their shoelaces or put on their shin guards. As soon as Gina spots me, she starts sniffing loudly like a stray pit bull catching a whiff of raw steak.

She takes an extra deep breath in, slowly exhales, and says, "Mmmmmmm-hmm. I smell victory."

I check over both of my shoulders real quick to make sure I am in the clear to bolt if necessary, then I snap freely: "That must just be your own feet you're smelling, Sardine-Toes. Cuz victory doesn't reek that bad."

My teammates chuckle.

It takes her a minute to understand that she's been owned. Gina glares at me for making everyone laugh at her expense. She looks like she's searching for a comeback, but girlfriend is more brawn than brains.

"Oh yeah? Well, my foot's gonna smell even worse after I kick your butt, Monty-neeeeeegro."

The attempt to insult my race and skin color turns out to be a self-own. The muffled snickers around me prove me right. Flustered, Gina clod-hops toward me, and I puff out my chest and stand tall like the proud Taino warrior I am. Just then, Kayla moves through the small crowd of players to stand beside me, and her tall presence makes my heart swell.

"Just you wait, Maya. I'll be waitin' for ya in the penalty box," Gina threatens as she walks backward to her team's sideline. "I'ma take you out, gurl."

On any given game day, Coach instructs us to remove all jewelry before taking to the field. No one wants to see an earlobe ripped up (or in one girl's case, a nostril) or a finger turn blue. But I leave the azabache on under my uniform— just in case. If there's one thing I know I can use protection from, it's Gina's wrath. And she seems like she's on one today.

Just before kickoff, I touch the azabache through my uniform. It feels red-hot. We take our positions on the pitch. As soon as the whistle blows, I pass the ball behind me to Kayla. My adrenaline kicks in as she dribbles the ball up the left side of the field and I jog alongside her, prepping for the next pass. Game faces on.

After a grueling first half, the Honey Badgers are ahead 1–0, thanks to a bad bounce off the goalpost. I am frustrated with myself, cuz I've made about eight shot attempts and had at least five potential assists, but Gina has managed to block every single one. I also spent the first half getting barraged by Gina's cackles and insults:

"You got NO game, Montenegro! Nada! None!"

"You think that weak shot is gonna drop in the net? HA! HA!"

"Puh-lease! My grandmama can kick harder than that!"

"Better luck next time . . . NOT!"

"Whatsa matta? You 'fraid ta come any closer, Monty? I'm waaaaiiiting . . ."

With seven minutes left in the second half, the score hasn't changed. Neither team is showing any sign of weariness. But with each last ticking minute, I become more and more determined—and it isn't just Ini and Mini's cheesy off-key cheers egging me on from the sidelines.

"Vámonos, Warriors! Go, go, go."

"Goooooo, Maya! Kick that goal . . . in the . . . goal!!"

I wait for the throw-in with hands on my haunches, gulping as much air into my lungs as I can. Jacqui revs up just out of bounds near the penalty line and throws in the ball to Kayla, who traps it with her chest, and then seamlessly bounces it from her knee to her foot. As she starts dribbling, I shuffle forward along centerfield, until I see two fullbacks try to charge Kayla. That's when I see the opening up ahead. I bolt up-field full blast, careful not to go offsides. Kayla reads my mind, cuz she taps the ball at a sharp enough angle for me to catch up to it.

Meanwhile, Gina is squatting like a sumo wrestler in the goalie box, poised to pounce on anything that comes her way. She lunges forward and tries to intercept the pass. But my quickness proves too much for her, as I trap the ball and dribble it outside of the penalty box.

Frustrated, Gina barks at her defenders to guard the goal. She is coming after me directly. I step on the ball, and quickly back-pass it with my heel to Jacqui behind me. The Honey Badger fullbacks are thrown off-pace, and Gina herself is caught out wide.

I sprint to the goal line. Jacqui floats the perfect lob into the air—my cue to go Air Maya, leaping into the air to head the ball . . . and *SWOOSH!* into the net.

But I wasn't counting on being taken down.

Microseconds after my head grazes the soft leather on the ball, Gina body-slams me. Tumbling as an entangled unit, our bodies crash together on the grass. Then, on her way up, she gives me a strong kick with her cleat into my stomach, which launches me headfirst into the goal post.

My eyes flutter, struggling to stay open. Shooting pain in my head and my gut. I hear the crowd going wild, and then a collective gasp. I touch the azabache as my eyes get heavier. It is cool again, as if it did its job. Still, I pass out.

Chapter 9

Back to Life, Back to Reality

WHEN MY EYES flutter open, a circle of folks is gathered around me—a rainbow of mixed team colors—royal-blue-and-white, black-and-red, and zebra-striped-ref jerseys all looking down on me with concern. I give them a faint smile to show them that I'm OK. Kayla is kneeling next to me and holding my hand. I squeeze it for reassurance.

She tells me, "You were out for fourteen seconds. I counted."

I glance sideways—out of the corner of my eye, I can see Gina nonchalantly twirling around the goal post, kicking the divots in the grass with her cleats.

I shift my focus to Coach, who is hovering over me.

"Wha' happened?" I ask bleary-eyed.

"You tied the game, took a pretty nasty tackle, and there's a bump on your forehead from sliding into the goal post," Coach says. "I thought you broke your neck! We've already called your mom. Can you wait for her to get here, or should I call the ambulance?"

My eyes widen with alarm. I shoot up, ignoring the throbbing from my head. "No, no. Tio Fausto said that unless we were bleeding to death, not to call for an ambulance. Too much money."

"Well, you need to get to the hospital," Coach says. He lays me back down to rest.

"Hospital?" I try to resist the pressure from his hand on my shoulder. "Why would I need to go there?"

"To make sure you don't have a concussion. That's the protocol."

"Concussion? Nah, I don't have a concussion," I say, touching the bump on my noggin. Maybe I shouldn't be so sure . . .

"Maya, you need to get checked out," he says. "This is the second instance this year. You had one during summer league, remember? If it is a concussion, you're gonna have to sit out for a while. Don't worry: Kayla can take the penalty kick."

Kayla looks at me apologetically and squeezes my hand. "It wasn't my idea," she says.

That's when I perk up and sit up. Our hands separate. I try not to look disappointed, but I'm fired up.

"Huh? Penalty kick? What penalty kick?"

Quickly, he snaps out of concerned-coach mode to competitive-coach mode and jumps up. "Yeah. You think Sardino can get away with that body check? No way! That should be a red card! This is girls' intramural soccer, not the WWE!"

"Coach, I want to take the kick," I say, dusting the dried grass off my arms and legs to prepare myself.

"Maya, no way. You've done enough for the team already. Besides, your mom is on her way. She'll have my butt on a platter if I let you play. Kayla, get in there."

Kayla leans back on her haunches and puts her hands up as if to surrender. "I don't think you can talk Maya out of this," she tells Coach. "This is personal now."

"Fine, OK, OK. Take the kick," Coach says. "But then you're going to the hospital to get checked out. Deal?"

"Deal."

"But do it quickly, before your mom arrives and tackles *me* to the ground," he adds as he walks back to the sideline.

After Ini and Mini help me up, I adjust my ponytail and my uniform while everyone takes their places, and the ref places the ball on the line.

I back up and give Gina a long, hard look. She doesn't look the least bit sorry, squatting and rubbing her hands together as if sitting down to Thanksgiving dinner, and the soccer ball a big ol' Butterball turkey. But right now, she is going to feel my left foot of fury.

Meanwhile, no one notices the dark storm cloud crawling across the sky and starting to hover over the field.

Ref blows the whistle. I take a deep breath and start my lopsided jog toward the ball, holding my left foot as long as possible, hoping Gina will commit to a direction.

My wish is granted. Gina leans right, so I turn my foot out wide and aim for the left corner. I kick it square and flat, and the ball takes flight and makes a dramatic SWOOOOOSH into the back corner of the net.

Adding an exclamation mark to my goal is a huge clap of thunder, followed by a massive downpour of rain: huge drops that send everyone who's cheering for my goal to run for cover—except something, or someone, is compelling me to stay put. Kayla runs over to me.

"Maya, come on!" she says, pulling on my jersey.

Instead, I just stand there, welcoming the drops that are hitting my face. The water feels . . . healing. The wind kicks up, and it's almost as though it's swirling around me, trying to lift me up. I put my arms out and lift my head toward the skies. The water feels so inviting, so warm, like a life force is wrapping itself around me when . . .

I feel a sudden tug on my wrist. I shudder back into consciousness. Oh, snap. It's Mami.

"Maya! ¿Qué falta contigo? What's wrong with you? You should be laying down, and I find you still playing? Out here in the rain? I ought to give you and that crazy coach of yours a cocotazo!"

Mami shields me with an umbrella and drags me away. Kayla runs for cover. Salma gallops alongside me and calls for Ini and Mini to hurry up. Mami hisses, "Vámonos! You want pneumonia on top of your concussion? I'm taking you to the hospital ahorita."

I can't stop grinning, even as Mami shoves me along. Trini hails a minivan taxi to take us all to the hospital.

Final score: Warriors—two, Honey Badgers—one. But more importantly: Maya—one, Gina—a big, fat, smelly zero.

Chapter 10

Mami's Furrowed Brow

As any Latina mother does, Mami imagines the worst has happened to her baby girl. The crease of worry between her eyebrows has been constant—from the time she picked me up at the field, the whole ride in the taxi, and all during our jail time—ahem, I mean, our wait in the ER.

Despite Mami's furrowed brow, I, on the other hand, am wrestling with the suspicion that the azabache saved me from a more serious injury, and that somehow, the raindrops healed me. After all, I'd survived a kick to the stomach and a head slide into a goalpost. I should be unconscious on a stretcher! But here I am in one piece, even if I am scraped up and soggy.

I excuse myself to go to the bathroom (on Mami's orders, Trini dutifully accompanies me). Once I am alone in the stall, I take off the azabache and stash it in my pocket to hide it, in case Mami knows its origin. But when I return to the waiting room, I can't help but rub the stone inside my pocket as if to summon the source of its mystical energy.

Sitting two-and-a-half hours in the waiting room is exhausting, but Mami keeps slapping my face to keep me from falling asleep. She is convinced that I will slip into a coma or something. Ini and Mini are practicing some new choreography, and Trini pulls out her sketchbook and starts drawing.

Finally, my name is called and we are escorted to a room, where we all crowd in. (We take this family togetherness seriously!) A few minutes after the nurse leaves, our boredom is rewarded by a handsome resident. His identification badge says "Jamal Benson, Medical Student" on it. His presence instantly perks all the girls up, and even though the twins try to suppress their giggles, I can tell they are playing "Spot the Hottie" telepathically.

Trini steps to him, as if Mami wasn't even there as my legal guardian. You know, the person who spent thirty-five hours in labor with me? (I'll never live that down.)

"Hello, Dr. Benson. My name is Trinidad Calderon, and this is my niece, Maya Montenegro. She just had a nasty accident."

"It's Jamal, at least for now. But yes, I heard," he says. "You're the soccer stud, huh?" Jamal asks me. Not her. Me.

"Yeah, I guess. I scored both goals though." I try to sound modest, but sometimes it's just hard.

"Wow! That is impressive! A regular Abby Wambach!"

Mami with the furrowed brow takes center stage again: "Jamal, my daughter was knocked down to the ground, and hit her head on the goal post."

"Oh, and don't forget . . ." Trini starts . . .

"The kick to the stomach," Ini and Mini say together.

"Geez!" exclaims the doctor in training. "Were you playing soccer or arena football?"

He takes my vitals, just like the nurse did minutes before, and scribbles in my chart.

Mami says, "They said she was unconscious for one whole minute!"

"It was only fourteen seconds, Ma," I correct her. I smile, remembering that Kayla was the one counting.

"Bueno, remember you had another concussion about three months ago," Mami adds.

"Mmm-hmmm. Well, Mrs. Montenegro, that's just the body's way of avoiding pain. But we're going to run a CAT scan to make sure, because concussions are serious business. There are nearly four million sports-related concussions a year. Whenever there is a blow to the head, the brain basically bounces within the skull, which can stretch and damage brain cells."

"Ay, Señor," Mami mutters, making the sign of the cross.

"Now, I'm not trying to scare you, but since this is your second incident in three months, we have to take extra precautions, Maya."

Jamal shines his pen light into my eyes and I squint. "Hmmmm, a little light sensitivity. Any dizziness?"

"Nope," I answer.

"Nausea?"

"Nuh-uh."

"Who was the first President of the United States?"

"George Washington." This feels like the world's easiest quiz.

"Beyoncé or Rihanna?"

"Uh, Lizzo?" I respond.

Jamal flashes a bright smile, then pats on the seat of the nearby wheelchair. "Now, you, hop down and park your keester, seester, and I'll have the nurse take ya on up."

"Uh, Jamal?" Trini pipes up again.

"Yes?"

"Should someone perhaps accompany her?"

"If you'd like, Miss, uh . . ."

"Calderon. Trinidad Calderon. I'm Maya's aunt. We're very concerned, you know." Trini is trying so hard to sound mature, yet coquettish. So ridiculous. But Jamal seems to have fallen for it. Men always do.

"Yes, I understand completely, Miss Calderon. It's not necessary, but if Maya wants . . ."

"No, Maya doesn't want," I answer quickly. "I'm OK, my dearest Auntie. *Really.* Don't you worry your frizzy little head about me."

Trini self-consciously presses her hand to her hair to smooth it. Got her.

While I am being whisked away for a CAT scan—you know, for possible signs of actual brain damage—Triflin' Trini somehow manages to put on a fresh coat of lipstick and spritz some perfume on her neck. Nice to know she is so concerned for my health and well-being. But Mami is doing enough worrying for the whole lot of us. She keeps checking my forehead for a trace of a fever, or to see if my pupils are becoming dilated, or something like that.

I push her hands away to keep her from fussing over me. "Mami, stop it! You don't think the doctors checked everything already? I'm telling you, I'm *fiiiine.*"

"I don't understand why you girls don't wear helmets in this game," Mami says.

"Mami, that's loca!"

"It's not crazy. Well, we'll just see what the doctor says. ¿Y dónde está él?"

"Here I am," Jamal says as he makes a second entrance. An older, white doctor shadows him. Did he get handsomer while he was gone?

"Wow! You know Spanish too?" Trini marvels.

"Un poquito," he says with a heavy American twang. "Did the obligatory two years in high school. I just stick to the basics."

"Well, your accent is good," Trini lies, to boost his ego. He flashes another bright smile. My eyes can't roll any harder.

"Doctor, what about my daughter?" Mami turns to Jamal's supervisor pleadingly.

Leave it to Mami to cut to the chase. I hold my breath. If I do have a concussion, I'll be out, possibly for the season.

"I'll let Jamal handle this," says the doctor.

Jamal clears his throat. "Well, I hate to be the bearer of bad news, but it is, in fact, a mild concussion," he says. "No sports for seven to ten days."

"But what about the game next Saturday?" I plead.

"Sorry, kiddo. You gotta sit this one out. It could've been a lot worse. You could've arrived here in a coma. You must have a guardian angel or something."

My face falls. I stare down at my feet to keep myself from crying. Soccer is my passion, and I know my teammates will be counting on me.

Salma actually looks sad for me, and Mami puts her arm around me.

"It's OK, Maya. It's just one game," Salma says to comfort me.

"Yes, just take it easy," says Jamal. "If you start to feel any pain, just take two ibuprofen every four hours. You can ice that bump on your noggin. And if you feel dizzy or nauseous, you can always come back to the ER if you can't get to your regular doctor. Unless you have any other questions for me . . . you're free to go."

"Thank you for taking such good care of us, Jamal," Trini says while slowly stretching out her hand, like the diva she is. Carajo, maybe things were better during the height of the coronavirus pandemic, when we went without all this touchy-touchy stuff.

Jamal takes her hand. "De nada." Again, with the gringo accent.

"You should stop by Café Taza sometime. We'll hook you up with a good criollo meal." She places her other hand on top of his. Boy, Trini has put a spell on the doctor in training.

He smiles. "Maybe one of these days I'll take a break from cafeteria food. Anyway, y'all take care." Jamal gently pulls his hand away and he and the doctor walk out.

I'm pretty sure everybody left the ER swooning except for Mami and me.

ON THE CAB RIDE home, Trini scrolls through her Instagram while Mami speaks to Papi on the phone, explaining what just happened to his estrellita.

"Uh, Maya." Trini says, handing me her phone. "You might want to see this . . ."

Chapter 11
Marvelous Maya

By Sunday morning, the video has gone viral. When Kayla emailed me Nestor's post about me, it already had more than four thousand likes and over two hundred comments. First, it shows Gina knocking me out. Then, cut to me, hitting the penalty kick. The caption: "TFW you try to take down Marvelous Maya. #swish" He follows it up with three heart-eye emojis. Ugh. Ugh. Ugh.

Mami insists I not work at the café and rest at home. Even though I do twenty-five pushups in front of her, she says she still doesn't trust a diagnosis from a medical student in his twenties. I plop myself down at the kitchen table in defeat.

But before Mami leaves for the café, she whips up a hearty breakfast for Salma and me, complete with eggs, panqueques, and bacon—my three favorite food groups. Mami kisses me on the forehead and dashes out.

I am merrily scarfing down the contents of my plate when Salma comes downstairs, sees me in my pajamas, and immediately starts sourpussing through my special treatment.

"Oh, of course you get to stay home and get a custom-made breakfast!" she says.

"It's for you, too, Sal. So don't complain," I say with my mouth full of syrupy pancakes.

But Salma isn't buying it. First, I kick the winning goal. Then, I go viral. Now, I milk the sympathy of being injured and don't have to work the brutal Sunday brunch shift.

"Look, Sal. Mami left a note for you." I've already read it. My sister isn't going to be happy about this. Still, I relish the moment.

"Salma, be a good hermanita and work the coffee station at brunch."

Salma groans and crumples up the Post-It. "Aw, man! Not only do I have to hear of how Marvelous Maya miraculously won the soccer game and escaped physical harm, like you're some sorta superhero, but now I gotta work the coffee station cuz you're allowed to stay home?!?"

"Sorry, Sal. Dem's da breaks." I shrug before stuffing a mouth full of eggs. Just to be a jerk, I add, "Hmmmm . . . Marvelous Maya. Kinda has a nice ring to it, don't it?"

Salma swipes a strip of bacon, gnaws a bite off, and storms out of the kitchen with a frustrated growl. A few seconds later, I hear the front door slam shut. I shrug my shoulders and grab the bacon she left behind.

After I clear my plate, I scramble upstairs and jump back into bed. I wince a little as I land, realizing that I do have some scrapes and a couple of bruises forming on my legs and arms.

OK, so Marvelous Maya isn't totally invincible. I ease myself under the covers a little more gingerly.

I am old enough now to stay home by myself, but it isn't such a major deal anywhoo, being close to the café.

Plus, I know for a fact that I will be paid a post-brunch-time visit by either Mami or Abuela, toting a to-go container filled with a tummy-warming meal from the café.

I hunker down under the covers, grab my book off the nightstand, turn on my playlist on my laptop, and bounce my head to the beat of the music until I nod off.

About three o'clock, the sound of the front door of our brownstone unlocking wakes me up.

"Mami? Is that you?" I call downstairs.

"No, m'ijita. It's Abuela. I bring you some black bean soup and pollo asado," she calls back upstairs.

"Who made the chicken?" I ask as I make my way down the hallway.

"I make, cómo no," she says, sounding almost insulted. "You think I no cook for my sick nieta?"

I savor her compliment then scurry down the stairs barefoot and into the open arms of my grandmother, practically barreling her over in the process.

"Gracias, Abuelita," I say. That woman can throw down in the kitchen almost as well as Mami.

"Ay, de nada, mi nieta preciosa," she beams. She frowns a little as she examines my face closely and adds, "I hear you take a nasty accident."

"Naaaaaah," I say. "You know Mami—she's just a big worrywart." I lead her by the shoulders into the kitchen to feed me.

"Ay, sí. Es verdad," she says as she unpacks the goodies. "My daughter no get that attitude from me. You are like me: a rough cookie."

"You mean tough cookie," I correct her with a laugh. "And you bet, Abuela."

I take a seat at the counter, and she starts to regale me with one of her great stories from her days as a dancer. "Oye, I remember many years ago, when your Abuelo and I perform in San Juan at a dance tournament. It was the finals, and he want to try this lift we only do in practice one time before. I say, 'OK, Chucho, but you better not drop me.' And he say, 'Not on my life, mi amor.' He lift me, up and over his head, and—FUÁCATA!" she exclaims, with a smack of her hand for emphasis. "I land flat on my back."

"Omigosh! What happened?" I ask, my eyes wide.

Abuela serves me a bowl of black bean soup and scoops a dollop of sour cream on top for a taste of extra-creamy goodness. Aaahhh, just the smell of the cilantro, garlic, and onions makes me warm and tingly all over before taking even one spoonful—a different kind of brujería if you think about it.

"Pues, I go unconscious por dos minutos. Finalmente, when I wake up, I am on—¿cómo se dice?—un stretcher. And my arms go out like this," she pauses, holding her arms out like Frankenstein, "and I go to strangle your grandfather!"

I giggle along with her. I love the way she rolls her r's when she says *estrrrrrrrrrangle*.

It's hard to believe this woman, who has so much generosity and love in her heart, can breed such contempt for her own sister. Actually, maybe with all the beef between me and Salma these days, I can relate after all. And maybe that sibling rivalry is the key to everything . . . ?

"¿Abuela?"

"¿Sí, m'ijita?" Abuela has an eager-to-please look on her face.

Now is the perfect chance. I want to pry the truth out of her so badly I can taste it. I dip my spoon into the black, creamy potion and blow before laying the groundwork for my way in.

"Ummmm . . . I don't know how to say this, but . . . I think I hate Salma."

"What kind of tontería is that?" she asks. She pulls out a small cleaver from a cabinet drawer and sets it on the counter.

The trap is set.

"You know, that girl, she's just always so darn moody. Personally, I think she's mad jealous of me."

"Pues, m'ijita, of course she going to be jealous of you," she says as she starts pulling the chicken from the bone. "All hermanitas look up to their big sisters, always wondering how in the world they can be more like them, without having to ask for permission," she replies. "That's how it was between your Mami and your tía."

AHA!!!! My plan is working beautifully so far. I just need to go back one more generation. I approach the next question with caution:

"Um . . . Was that how it was between you and your sister, Yaya?"

There is a long pause . . . until the SMACK of the wooden spoon on the kitchen counter breaks the silence. I flinch, hoping that spoon won't make its mark somewhere on my nalgas next.

Abuela hisses through her teeth, pointing the spoon at me. "No! Do NOT mention the name of that woman in this house, or any other house in this family. Ever. ¿Entiendes?"

"Abuelita, come on. You can't be serious. This is me, Maya. Your oldest grandchild. I'm not a baby anymore. You can't pull a fast one over me," I say. "What did she ever do to deserve to be banished to the apartment above the café? She's family!"

"Primero, m'ija, granddaughters no speak to their abuelas like that. You are to show respect." She picks up the cleaver to start deboning the chicken.

"But I just want . . ."

"Eh! Eh! Eh! ¡Ni una palabra! Not one more word," she barks, emphasizing each word by taking the cleaver to the chicken carcass. That poor pollo.

"But that's not fair, Abuela! You tell me I'm not allowed to hate my sister but then you're allowed to pretend yours doesn't even exist? That sounds like a hypocrite's double talk to me."

I make sure I stay on my side of the kitchen counter. These are bold words suddenly coming out of my mouth.

"¿Qué? ¿Qué? ¡Ipócrita? ¡¡¿Ipócrita?!? This is how you show respect? ¡No! I no have to answer to you. Es *mi* casa." Abuela is heated now.

"But this is my family! I have a right to know!" I exclaim.

She puts the knife down (thankfully) and comes to my side of the counter. "Oye, let me tell you something: children have no rights. That is the problem with your generation—you think the world owes you something todo el tiempo!" She points a finger in my face.

"Oh yeah? Well, the problem with *your* generation is that you bottle everything bad up inside you until it rots and rots and eats you alive!" I hop off the stool, in case I need to make a break for it.

"Ay, nena," she says in frustration. "I no can have this conversation with you. When you are more old you maybe understand . . ."

That is my trigger phrase. I throw up my hands in frustration.

"Maybe when I'm older?! Why is that the ultimate excuse for everything in this house? And now, I come to you, my only grandmother in the whole world, to ask about my own family history, and you give me the same old tired excuse! I'm thirteen now! How 'old' do I have to be to understand my family history?"

"Sí, m'ija, I don' know exactamente. But you are still a child. And you . . ."

Abuela stops whatever she was about to say. She is staring right at my chest.

After coming home from the ER, I had put the aza-bache back on and tucked it under my shirt. But at that moment, with me wearing a pajama tank top, it is in plain view. The azabache certainly isn't saving me from Abuela's version of el mal ojo right now. It's easy to see where Mami and Salma inherited that look from.

"¿Qué es eso? Why are you wearing that . . . that . . . *thing* around your neck?" she asks.

I shrug my shoulders in petulant defiance. "I found it. I liked it. I wore it."

"¡Mentirosa!" she says, shaking in anger. "Why must you lie to me on top of disrespecting me like this?"

"I didn't mean . . ." I clutch the azabache defensively.

"¿Ella te lo dio? Did she give it to you?" Abuela doesn't even dare utter the woman's name. She just waves her hand in the general direction of the restaurant.

I want her to say it though. "Who?"

"Esa bruja . . ."

"You mean your sister, Yaya? Is that who we're talking about? The one who is a witch? I thought we weren't supposed to talk about her in the house . . ."

I don't know where this boldness is coming from, but it's almost as though I can't help myself now.

"¡Ay! Answer me the question, Maya Beatriz Montenegro Calderon. ¿Esa bruja te lo dio? ¿Eh? ¿Eh?"

After hearing my full name being called, I know this is serious. Abuela is full-on losing it.

"I-I-I . . . I don't know, Abuela. I woke up and it was there. Honest!" I touch the stone again, hoping it will save me from Abuela's wrath.

"¡Ay, mentirosa! ¡Basta! I no understand why you must continue to lie to me! Desgraciada . . ."

I've never seen my grandmother go off like this. I decide to back down.

"I-I-I'm sorry, Abuela, but I'm not lying. That's really what happened . . ."

"Dámelo."

"But Abuela . . ." I plead.

"¡Dámelo!" she repeats.

I begrudgingly take the azabache off and place it in her outstretched hand.

"Oye, m'ija. I will only tell you this once: Déjala—you stay away from that woman. She has already caused enough trouble in this family to last me a lifetime." She talks sternly, but she is choking back tears as she leaves me sitting in the kitchen, alone with my confused thoughts and my now-cold soup.

But I could've sworn I heard her mutter under her breath,

"I don't need to lose another to brujería . . ."

Another?

Chapter 12
Stirring the Pot

It's IRONIC: here I am, just a cute, curious kid, trying to get information about my family history out of my Abuela, an adult who clearly has the answers, and then when the pot finally stirs up and boils over, I'm the one feeling empty and uncomfortable inside.

Now I'm all alone in the house again. I go back upstairs to my room and fire up my laptop to log into my Gmail. I know it's old school, but without being allowed a cell phone until next year, all I have to connect to the outside world is email, G-Chat, and Google Meet. I am hoping there'll at least be an email waiting for me from Kayla or my cousin Taina in California, who's just four months younger than me.

Nope, the only new message waiting for me in my inbox is from Nestor Garcia, who had made it known to the entire world that he is still crushing on me with those three darn heart-eye emojis. Now he's asking how I am feeling. He really is sweet, despite everything.

Then I think of the dream that brought me the azabache, and of that strange word: aché. I decided to do a quick Google search. Let's see . . . there is stomachache, backache, toothache, heartache . . . American College of Healthcare Executives . . . nothing that even remotely looks Spanish, Taíno, or African, or Caribbean, or anything that could be attributed to my ancestors.

I figure I'll be pretty much left alone for the rest of the afternoon as the familia prepares for the dinner shift. Instead of watching Mami's telenovelas, I think maybe I am safe to seek an answer in person. And that person happens to own a bakery down the street.

I slip out of my PJs and throw on jeans, a dark blue T-shirt, some fresh kicks, and a baseball cap. I want to look as nondescript as possible, just in case I am spotted on the streets as I walk over to the Infante Bakery. The new people in the neighborhood just be nosey for no reason.

When I arrive, the place looks empty. I push the door open, and the bell jingles. Out comes Señora Infante, with fresh puffs of flour dusted on her chest.

"Maya, what are you doing here?" she asks. "¿Todo tranquilo?" She pats her bosom and flour clouds appear.

"Yeah, everything's cool," I say. I detect a hint of sadness in my voice, which I try to cover up with a crooked smile.

"You want a leche con café?" she offers without me having to ask.

"Sure, thanks," I say with a smile. "I appreciate your keeping my budding coffee habit a secret."

Señora Infante chuckles. "Eh, it's only a matter of time before we all fall in love with the cafecito." She grabs a to-go cup and starts spooning sugar in the cup. "Why aren't you at the café?" she asks.

"Oh, Mami made me stay home today," I answer.

"Ay, sí. She told me this morning about your soccer accident. ¿Cómo te sientes?" she asks as she pours the milk into coffee and stirs.

"I feel fine, actually. That's why I'm here." I plop down at the counter.

She gave a knowing grin as she hands me the cup. "Aaah, sí. El azabache. I suppose it proved to be quite useful for you then?"

"Yeah, I guess you're right. But I don't have it anymore. Abuela took it." I stare at my cup wistfully.

"I see," she replies slowly. "Bueno, would you like unas galletas?"

My face lights up. "Yes, please." That sounds divine.

I feel like I'm in a safe space. I want so badly to confide more in her. To tell her everything that's happened to me so far. And yet, I still start out with a lie.

"Señora, I'm doing a research project for school," I say. "Umm . . . do you know what something called aché is? I've looked it up in the dictionary, I went online and everything, and I can't find it anywhere. I don't even know if I'm spelling it right."

Señora Infante tries to stifle her laugh, but her belly gives her away. She places a small plate with three still-warm cookies on it.

"Why do you ask about the aché, Maya, dear? Has someone accused you of having it?" she asks with a knowing grin. She walks behind the counter.

"I dunno . . . Maybe . . . I'm not sure, really." I dip my cookie into my coffee drink and take a bite to avoid any further explanation of my crazy dreams.

"Pues, m'ija, you cannot look it up, because you must look inside to find it."

"Huh?" I almost do a spit take at her directness.

Señora Infante reaches across the counter and points a thick finger directly at my heart. "It is in here." She traces the air around my body frame. "And it is out here—all around you." She gestures broadly.

"Oh, I see," I say, trying not to give my clueless face away.

She looks directly at me. "Mira, aché is an ancient Yoruba word that represents life energy. It is a force that is not of this earth. Aché is something we cannot measure. It must first be awakened. Those who answer their aché are truly blessed. Those who have it and never know it's there, their life's purpose goes wasted . . ."

She shakes her head. There is a deliberate pause, as if she wants me to soak in her words. Then she continues:

"Like a blanket, aché wraps around you. And sometimes, if you are chosen by an orisha, your aché has the power to affect others. It is quite a special gift to have the aché."

"What is an orisha? And how do you get chosen?" I ask.

Señora Infante moves her attention to the rest of the galletas on the cookie sheet. She begins sprinkling powdered sugar on the cookies. "They are deities of the Regla Lucumí. Orisha means 'owner of your head.' Each orisha has a different personality and acts like a guardian angel to whoever their chosen children are. An orisha chooses you based on your traits and your personality. For many, it is a natural gravitation."

"Is it like a cult or something?" I take a bite of cookie in anticipation of her response and chew slowly.

"No, no, no," she says, dismissing my tontería. "It is not like that at all. It is simply a way of life that our

Yoruba ancestors have passed down from generation to generation."

This is heavy stuff. But for some reason, it all makes sense to me. But then I wonder: Have I actually been chosen by a goddess?

I take a long sip of my coffee before posing another question: "Do you know if my Titi Yaya is a witch for real? That's what Abuela says."

"Ay, no, Maya," Señora Infante says, shaking her head to dismiss the silly rumors. "I knew her on the island. Yaya is known as a curandera—a healer. She is quite famous in our home village of Bayamón for her healing powers and her gift of seeing the future. People would come from all over Puerto Rico just to be blessed by her."

"Reeeeally? I'm related to someone else famous?" I ask, my eyes widening.

"Oh, sí. Your Abuela and Abuelo are not the only celebrities in your family," she says proudly.

"So then why is Titi Yaya banned from the family?"

The señora pauses putting the cookies in the display case to look at me. "Maya, out of respect for your family,

I cannot say. I have already said too much. In time, I trust that all will be revealed to you."

Then, she comes closer to me. In a whisper reserved for speaking in church, she says, "She'll be waiting for you on Friday night."

"Huh? Who?"

She gives another belly laugh and says, "Ya tú sabes." She adds with a wink, "You see, I have the aché too."

"You do?" I gasp, impressed. "I didn't realize you got down like that, Señora Infante!"

"Eh," she says with a self-deprecating shrug. "I have just enough to recognize it in others." She wipes her hands on a dish towel. "But yours? Ay . . . muy fuerte. I can see how strong it is. It would be a shame to waste it. Like . . ." Señora Infante tightens her lips to stop herself.

Before I can get too curious, we are interrupted by the sleigh bell on the door. A thirty-something male customer bursts in with a last-minute order: "Pleeeease tell me you have baguettes left. My wife will kill me if I don't bring some home."

That's my cue to leave. I merely thank the señora and head out.

But I am beginning to see everything in a different light now. Imagine, having a famous aunt and an ancient African goddess choose you! That's pretty cool. I just need to keep digging to solve this puzzle.

Chapter 13

Gimme el Bochinche

ON MONDAY AT SCHOOL, everybody is still doling out the bochinche about how Gina Sardino tried to put me on the disabled list. And even though I blacked out, how I'd scored not one, but two goals in her face to make her gag on the loss. Seems like everybody in the neighborhood has had beef with Gina at one point in their lives. While regaling others with the tale, they'd mention as an aside, "And hey, wasn't that a weird thunderstorm that came outta nowhere?"

I have a sneaking suspicion the two events were related. My connection to all things water-related has become too obvious to ignore: at the beach, in my dreams, on the soccer field. The walls of my room that heralded the sea. All the different shades of blue clothes that occupy my closet. Today, I am wearing a periwinkle top with faded jeans that have holes in the knees.

As I walk down the hallways, I get daps and high fives, and hear myself being called "Sardine Killer." I feel like a New York Yankee after winning the World Series, minus the ticker tape parade.

At lunch, Kayla finds me. "Maya, how are you feeling? I was so worried!" she asks after hugging me. OK, post-coronavirus hugs are good after all.

"I'm fine. It's like I never had a concussion in the first place," I assure her.

I wish I could tell her about the azabache protecting me from a worse injury, but I feel like I can't tell another soul what is happening to me until I really figure it all out. Magic stones? Healing rain? She'd probably think I'm loca for real.

After school, all of the Montenegro and Calderon kids walk into Café Taza and plop down in our usual yellow upholstered corner booth. Titi Julia greets us with kisses and five glasses of pineapple batidos. I suck down the creamy, fruity, icy goodness through my straw. Being in the restaurant with family and food really is better—and cheaper—than putting all five of us in an after-school program.

"Your mom's making a fresh batch of tostones. I'll have Trini bring them out in a few," Titi Julia says.

Ten brown eyes widen at the prospect of those fried, crispy plátanos. When doused with mojo—a sauce of fresh ground garlic, olive oil, and vinegar—tostones are a snack way better than French fries or Doritos or potato chips. It is always a losing battle to see who can pop the most of those tasty treats in their mouth before the plate clears off—which usually clocks in about forty-two seconds flat.

As soon as Titi Julia leaves the table, my cousins start doling out their own bochinche:

"Yo, did you see the stank look on Gina's face when she passed by your locker today?" Ini announces, leaning forward.

"Clas-sick," Mini confirms.

"Yeah, uh-huh," I say, sipping mindlessly on my batido.

Frankly, I'm not in the mood for any more praise. I am still distracted by my convo yesterday with Señora Infante.

She told me those who answer their aché are truly blessed. Those who have it and never know it's there, their life's purpose goes wasted. Am I wasting my life away already at thirteen?

And to think, Titi Yaya, the woman from my sea dreams, is just upstairs, and I can't just walk through that kitchen and see her right now to get some answers . . .

"Yo, that Gina's got a serious case of the wackles," says Ini.

"Yeah, chica is dripping in wack juice," says Mini.

"I'd like some more juice, please. Wait. What does wack juice taste like?" asks Mo.

We all stop to laugh. Mo can always crack us up without him even knowing what a comedian he is.

"But yo, you made Sardino eat her words!" exclaims Ini.

"Every single one!" adds Mini.

"Yeah, yeah. Chalk one up for Maya Montenegro," I say flatly. I make a loud slurping noise through my straw.

"CHICKA . . ."

"POW!!" Ini and Mini chime in quick succession.

The twins even add hand gestures to it. They are so pleased with their spur-of-the-moment move, they slap each other with their signature choreographed dap afterwards.

Salma, who has been silently stewing this whole time, finally pipes up: "Yo, could we stop bragging about Marvelous Maya for like, three seconds today?"

We all jump back in our seats. But Sal isn't finished ranting.

"¡Carajo! I've, like, only had to hear it every minute of every day for the past two days straight now. Big deal, so what? You won a soccer game! Good for you! Enough already! ¡Basta ya!"

"Y'know what, Sal? I'm with you," I say, slamming my now-empty glass down for emphasis. "I'm tired of hearing about me too. Let's change the subject. How are your guitar lessons going?"

Salma looks shocked that I am actually agreeing with her . . . and asking about her.

"Oh, good! I'm learning how to pluck 'La Bamba,'" she says, beaming.

Just then, Trini exits of the kitchen and plops the plate of fried green plátanos in front of us. In typical boricua fashion, Ini grabs the glass jar of mojo and starts spooning the sauce over the tostones, while Mini picks up the salt shaker and starts shaking. No one seems to care that salt is being sprinkled onto their greedy little hands as they reach for the crispy yet chewy chips.

Just when I think I'm safe from the Wrath of Salma, Trini opens her big mouth.

"Maya, I just saw your video has more than seven thousand likes now. That's dope!"

"AAAAAAAAARRRRGH!!!" Salma screams and pounds her fists on the table. She gets up and stomps toward the kitchen. She quickly turns around to retrieve her batido and snatches a tostón, then turns on her heel and marches to the kitchen.

"What, what'd I say?" Trini asks innocently.

"Oh, nuthin' much—she's sick of hearing about me, y'know, same ol', same ol'," I answer. "Papi called last night and said he even saw the video."

But Trini's eyes are already wandering. She shifts her hips and turns her head to get a better look at the café's newest guest.

"Hey . . . hottie spotted," she mutters to us.

Aw, man! I am in no mood for Spot the Hottie right now. I'm on a fact-finding mission.

But the twins are always game. "Where?" They try not to look too obvious, but they're not very good at being subtle.

Trini points with her head. "At the counter. Blue cargo pants."

"Yeah, whatever," I say, as I use this opportunity to grab two tostones. The last thing I want to do is think about boys. I need answers. "Have you heard any good bochinche on our infamous Titi Yaya?" I ask, taking a bite.

"Huh? What . . . no, not really." Trini isn't paying attention to any of us, she is too busy sizing up Blue Cargo Pants. He is checking her out as well, until . . .

"Oh, hold up. He's wearing a nametag. An electronics salesman. Next," she says, sounding mad disappointed. She turns around, whisking her hand away in the air as if he would just disappear at her whim.

"Ouch!" says Ini. Chomp.

"That's cold," says Mini. Chomp.

"That's life," says Trini, shrugging her shoulders nonchalantly.

Just as she is about to take the now empty plate back to the kitchen, I say, "Excuuuuuuuse me, Titi Gold Digger." I pause for emphasis, knowing that will grab her attention.

When she raises an eyebrow at me, I shake a tostón at her, saying, "I was asking you the deal about Titi Yaya. What's the good word?"

"Nada mucho," she replies. "Not a whole lot of rumbling going on upstairs, family-wise, y'know? Abuela hasn't been up there since Yaya moved in. I've seen some folks go up there to visit her, though."

"Oh yeah? Like who?"

Trini puts the plate back down and leans in to whisper: "Like Jorge from the bodega. Oscar too!"

"Get out! Really?" I exclaim. This is good stuff. "Who else?"

"Rosario Infante." (I knew that one already.)

"Word?" said Ini.

"And Aracely from the hair salon," Trini says.

"What do they come for?" Mini asks.

"Dunno. But they all come out with a little brown bag."

"Like a lunch bag?" Mo pipes in.

"Yep." And Trini takes the plate and sashays away.

I decide right then and there that I need to sneak upstairs to see this viejita for myself. Friday night is when Señora Infante said Titi Yaya would be waiting for me. It might be busy enough that no one would notice if I slip away for a few minutes. So . . . Friday night it is.

Chapter 14

Full Moon Shenanigans

It not easy being sneaky in my familia. The minute you stop acting like your old self, out come the side eyes. And then, the questions:

"Ay, ¿qué te pasa?"

"Wassup witchu?"

"You got gas or something? Here, take some Tums."

On the whole, I keep my demands to a minimum for those few days. Obey Mami. Keep outta Salma's grill. Since I can't go to soccer practice this week, I finish my homework diligently, and even do the extra credit—in essence, I am doing everything to try to be the model daughter, sister, and student.

Even Abuelo Chucho, who almost never looks up from his intense sidewalk rivalries of dominoes against Jorge on the patio, raises a concerned salt-and-pepper eyebrow at me one afternoon. I distract him by pointing out the linebacker of a man walking down the street with a chihuahua that's wearing a tiny sweater. Siete hisses at the dog half his size and the toy-sized dog yips back, which causes her whole body to bounce backwards. I know this scenario will set Abuelo off on one of his mini-rants on how the neighborhood is changing.

"Used to be, people owned dogs to protect their home," Abuelo Chucho laments. "Now they fit in your hand. And wear clothes."

He watches the muscle man pick up puny pup turds.

"Who owns who now, eh? Eh?" he says aloud, then lets out a hearty guffaw. Jorge joins him in laughter. Siete perches himself on Jorge's lap and watches the dog suspiciously as she prances away.

Jorge assigns numbers to his cats instead of names, in an attempt to not get attached to them. After all, bodega cats are there to work—catching all the mice, rats, and cockroaches. But of course, Jorge can't help himself, especially now that he's older. Siete is his seventh cat since opening the bodega twenty-eight years ago—and each one is spoiled rotten. Oscar thinks his old man is making the cat lose his killer instincts. My family doesn't help matters either. We're like Siete's second family. Even though we're not allowed to have a pet of our own in the house ("Too much responsibility," Papi says), I'll catch Mami standing at the back door feeding Siete chicken gizzards, and we kids love to love up on him every chance we get.

I have to laugh too. "Used To Be" is one of my favorite games to play with Abuelo. (He already went off on the broccoli place earlier: "They serve it in a cup? Like ice cream? Only it's broccoli? Ay, esa gente . . ."

I kiss Abuelo's forehead, give Siete a neck scratch, and keep marching to the tune inside my head. After all, what I am about to risk could throw all that out the window— because from the sounds of it, my family could easily throw my pompis out on the streets, banned from the Calderon family altogether. I mean, if they are capable of holding an old lady practically a prisoner upstairs, what would they do to a disobedient teenager? I have a hard time reconciling that. Is that any way to treat our flesh and blood? What's to stop them from doing that to me? Could I possibly be shut out from the familia too?

My buena-nena act pretty much has everybody fooled—except for the ever-suspicious Salma. Every time I see her, she's giving me side eye, as if she's trying to catch me hatching some sort of mischievous plot. Once again, el mal ojo has successfully passed its way down to another generation of Calderon women. And I don't have the azabache anymore to protect me.

I just tell my little sister to mind her garbanzos and I go about my business. I really am working on my science project.

My project is about how the sun and moon affect the tides—which, given my own gravitation toward all things ocean-related (including in my dreams), doesn't seem like a coincidence. Tides are the result of forces colliding between the earth, moon, and sun. Even though the sun is huge, it's three hundred and sixty times farther away from earth than the moon is. And the moon's gravitational force is twice as strong on the tides as the sun, because of its proximity to earth. This tug-of-war between the sun and the moon pulls the earth's oceans into an elliptical shape, called a tidal bulge. As a result, water "piles up" in the oceans, which causes the high tide.

As the earth rotates, different parts of the planet are affected by the tidal bulge. This is what makes the tides rise and fall. And amazingly, the moon's gravity creates a high tide on both sides of the earth. As the moon's gravity pulls on the earth, it pulls water into a bulge on the side closest to it. Meanwhile, on the opposite side of the earth, another high tide is created by the moon pulling the earth away from the still water on that side. Due to global warming, the moon is slowly moving farther away from the earth—like at the pace of your fingernails growing, which also affects the tides. But the pull is strongest during full moons. (Yeah, I'm totally getting an A on this project.)

I look at the calendar, and sure enough: Friday night there will be a full moon. Though not scientific, strange things have been known to happen during full moons—mysterious cositas, like more babies being born. It has to be some kind of omen.

~ ~ ~

THE CAFÉ WAS PRETTY quiet all week, so the family is caught off guard by a sudden Friday night dinner rush. Tio Fausto makes all of us kids gather up our books and backpacks quickly and stash them in the back, to free up the extra booth.

We then assume our positions as the Latine minions: for the twins, Salma, and me, that means bussing tables, bringing out bread and refilling water, dishing out chips and salsa, and even making a few local deliveries to the people we know.

It's kinda sucky to have to work on a Friday night, especially after my adrenaline-charged, totally bugged-out week thus far. At least on the positive side, Tio Fausto lets us divvy up the tip jar at the end of the night, which could mean some fresh kicks or even a new outfit. But I'm thinking with maybe this week's tips, I'll check out the botanica.

At least that's what I keep telling myself as I wipe the sweat off my brow every five minutes. Don't ever get it twisted: the restaurant biz is hard work!

At one point, Salma mutters as she whisks by, "Hottie at Table Seven."

As far as I'm concerned, that could've been three minutes or thirty minutes ago. The hustle is bustling too much to look up and admire the scenery. But that isn't my priority right now.

To me, it seems like a good use of the mamarracho to make my getaway—upstairs to the forbidden apartment.

"Get 'em in, get 'em fed, get 'em out," Tio Fausto barks to shake me back into the moment.

Even Mo is caught up in the hullabaloo and begs to help out. Usually, he just stays at the back table coloring or putting together Legos. But after enough nagging, a frustrated Tio Fausto finally thrusts two baskets of tortilla chips in his little hands and points him exactly where to deliver to Tables Eight and Nine.

Mo beams and hoists the two baskets over his three-foot-ten-inch frame, trying his bestest to weave his way through the crowd.

Pero pobrecito never makes it past Table Seven.

A basket of corn chips catapults its way onto the head and lap of the chulito who is trying to enjoy his chuletas.

At that moment, we *aaaaallll* spot the hottie: Jamal Benson himself, the super cute resident with the dreamy eyes and scintillating smile who took care of me in the ER. Trini did tell him about the café. Is he here for her, or for the pork chops? Either way, I'm sure he hadn't planned on being showered by corn chips.

Tio Fausto, already at his wit's end, rubs the throbbing vein in his temple as his nostrils flare. Just before he can make a move to dole out a cocotazo to his son, Trini cuts him off at the pass.

She touches his shoulder gently, cooing in her most feminine of tones, "Don't worry, big brother. I'll smooth this one over."

She checks her reflection in the back of a spoon, and fluffs up her hair, before sashaying over to the man who is too fine to dine alone.

That's when I decide to make my move.

Chapter 15

Her Name
Is My Name Too

I ENTER THE KITCHEN as quietly as I can. Mami is
there—but she goes into a completely different kind of
trance when she's cooking under pressure. Pots and pans
get banged, and sometimes flung around. It's the only
time I ever hear her swearing, and even that's under her
breath. It's kind of funny, actually. Part of me wishes I
could help her to take the pressure off, but everyone always
says to let her be when she gets this way. So, I go back to
focusing on my mission. I'm able to tiptoe past her as she
hovers over the stove, stirring a pot like she's trying to
drown demons in it. I exhale slowly, then gently climb up
the staircase.

When I get to the top floor, I see that the apartment door is ajar—is Titi Yaya really expecting me like Señora Infante said? I inch my way in and close the door behind me. Candles are lit in every direction, lighting up the dim room like the moon and stars illuminate the night sky. The room smells like the Brooklyn Botanical Garden. Wafts of these aromas—what are they? Lavender, rose water, mint, cocoa butter?—all surround me, making my fears disappear. This place is small but cozy and even cute—not even close to the slaughterhouse that Trini had us picturing. I close my eyes and take another deep breath to take in all the aromas once again. Hard to believe there's a cacophony of noise going on in the café below. It feels like I'm a world away.

"Hola m'ijita," the woman coos in a raspy whisper.

There Titi Yaya stands in all her glory—in the flesh, in the present, in the moment—and I can't gather one gosh-darn palabrita. Am I dreaming again, I wonder? But with her bewitching emerald eyes gleaming at me, she reaches her delicate dark hand to touch my face, and I realize this is the real deal.

With her other hand, Titi Yaya pulls back a single stray silver dreadlock that has fallen out of her white and blue patterned head wrap, which makes her appear taller than her diminutive frame, which is draped completely in white with blue embroidery. Against this blank canvas are multicolored beads around her neck, and on her wrists are shiny, silver bangles that make a swishing sound as they slide up and down her forearm.

She motions for me to sit down in one of the two worn chairs with mismatched upholstery. Sparsely decorated, everything in the room looks secondhand or borrowed—but curated tastefully. But wow, the shower really *is* next to the kitchen sink.

"¿Parece como tus sueños?" she asks with a wry smile.

I nod as I continue to take everything in. Yeah, it does feel like one of my dreams—minus the beach, of course. I notice that against the far wall is a small altar, draped in blue velvet, and there are white and blue candles that help light the room like undulating waves.

Titi Yaya smiles, takes a few steps, and she's in her kitchenette. She turns on one of the burners on the small stove and places a tea kettle. She starts humming. She takes another couple of steps and goes to the window, where a planter's box is sprouting all types of leaves and flowers on the fire escape. She picks a couple of sprigs of mint and places them into the teacups and pours boiling water from the whistling kettle. I am trying to place the tune she's humming. It sounds vaguely familiar . . .

Titi Yaya hands me a teacup and makes direct eye contact with me. "Do you know the song I sing?"

I start to shake my head no, but as she stares intently at me, I slowly kinda nod yes too.

Wait a momentito! The music box! It's the tune from the music box!

She grins knowingly. "That music box is mine. I pass to your Titi Dolores, and she pass to you. I sing your tía to sleep with that oriki, a praise song," she explains as she takes a seat in her kitchenette. There are a dozen white roses in a deep blue vase, brightening up the small, folding table. "When Dolores was baby, I rock her in my arms and sing that oriki to Yemaya to watch over her."

I sit across the table from her and peer into the teacup. There are all sorts of flowers and herb-type flakes floating in it, which smell good. I take a tiny sip.

"We do not have much time tonight, ya sabes," she cautions.

I nod. I realize I'm on borrowed time up here, yet there are at least a dozen questions swirling around in my head of all the things I don't know, which could fill this entire room.

If Titi Yaya gave Titi Dolores the music box, why did my aunt give it to me? Why am I having these janky thoughts and dreams? Why do I have this strange connection to water? Why has this woman chosen me to bestow her magical presence upon? Has she, in some way, been looking after me all these years? It's not like I was a neglected child or abandoned orphan or anything. I have relatives coming out my ears—why would I need a fairy godmother? And why me . . . why now?

Just as I'm half-wondering, half-hoping she can read my mind, Titi Yaya puts her hand on top of mine and breaks my stream of consciousness.

"Porque tú eres mi elegida," she says with a grin.

Apparently, she *can* read my mind. I'm her chosen one . . . ?

Wow. Wow. Wowzy wowzy woo.

Then she adds something I don't quite understand, "And because you are a daughter of Yemaya. She is calling you."

"¿Que qué? I thought I was the daughter of Soledad Calderon and Eduardo Montenegro, no? Please don't tell me I'm adopted . . ." I throw my head back and groan at the thought of another family secret being held from me.

"Ay, no," she chuckles, her narrow shoulders shaking up and down. "Mira, Yemaya is my orisha. Yemaya was orisha to Dolores too. But your tía did not answer the call."

"Orisha? I know that word! You mean a goddess, right?" Again, Señora Infante for the win.

"Sí. Yemaya is the goddess of the seas. She owns every drop of water on the earth." She gestures broadly in the shape of a globe.

"Every drop, huh? So that means the rain at the soccer match. The tides of the ocean. That was all her?" I ask.

"Exacto." Titi Yaya nods and smiles.

I pause to think, then ask, "So then why did I almost drown at Coney Island?"

Her face turns serious. "Because you are un iyabo—uninitiated. Sometimes, the call of Yemaya can be too strong for iyabos. You have dreams of her too, no?"

"Ooooh, yeah. I think so. I'm usually on the beach. I only see you, but I hear another woman's voice in the wind calling me. Is that her?"

"Sí. That is Yemaya Olokun. She appears in dreams to her children. You do not choose an orisha. An orisha chooses you. Why do you think your name is *Maya*?" Again with that wry, knowing smile.

"I thought it was for the Mayan Indians, to represent my Mexican heritage," I say, wondering if I've unearthed another family secret.

"Ay, that is what your proud Chicano father want you to think," she answers, shooing the thought away. "And that is true, but your name is short for Yemaya. Same as my name."

After a sip of her tea, she continues: "After Trinidad was born, I tell your mother that the next daughter born in the Santos family should be named after the goddess of the sea, to be protected. She promised me in secret."

"Santos?" I ask.

"Ay, they tell you nada of your history, your family," she says with a mild shake of her head. "Santos is my family name, your Abuela's—¿cómo se dice?—"

"Maiden name?"

"Exactamente. Mi apellido es Santos."

"Oh." So, my family's last name is literally Saints. More santería. This is getting heavy.

She gets up from her chair and takes the two steps back into the kitchen. "Oye, today is special. Not only is it a full moon, but September seventh is Yemaya's Feast Day. We must honor her. Come join me."

Titi Yaya tells me to take five of the white roses out of the vase and put the remaining seven on the altar. She then points to a candy dish of loose change and instructs me to take out seven shiny pennies and to place them on the altar as well. Meanwhile, she grabs a yam and banana from a basket on the counter and places them on the altar next to the roses. She takes three steps to get from the kitchen to the altar, and motions for me to do the same.

We both kneel on the two cushions that are on the floor in front of the altar. "Yemaya is the mother of all living things in West Africa and the Caribbean." She lights more candles. "She is the Goddess of the Living Ocean. She gave birth to the moon, sun, and stars, as well as all the other orishas. She is extremely protective of her children. But she is nurturing and loving."

Titi Yaya closes her eyes and opens her palms to the ceiling. I do the same.

She tells me, "Pray for strength. Pray for wisdom. You are a child of Yemaya and she is calling you. Let her show you the way."

I am not usually the praying type, but this seems like an important step in understanding what I'm going through. So, in my mind, I say "hey," and I ask the orisha to help me make sense of all this.

A few minutes later, Titi Yaya opens her eyes, stands up, and crosses over to her kitchenette. She pulls out the same large cauldron she unpacked the day I spied on her arguing with Abuela, and places it smack dab in the middle of the floor. She takes the cushion in front of the altar and moves it to the center of the room, crosses her legs, reaches in the cauldron, and pulls out a wooden cigar box. She takes out a cigar, chews off one end, and lights it with one of the large candles that are burning around her.

I try to hold back my giggles at the image of this petite old woman puffing on a big, stinky cigar. Whatever she is doing, she is being mad serious about it. I want to show respect, but I'm not sure exactly what I am witnessing.

Yaya takes out a güiro and starts to grind whatever mixture was inside with a mortar and pestle. Then she pours the powder into the cauldron. Then she motions for me to join her on the floor.

"Maya, no fear what you no know," she tells me, echoing the words from my dream, the words that I now know had been spoken to me by the orisha Yemaya herself. "What you no know will lead you to the path of knowledge."

She blows a puff of cigar smoke into the cauldron and then quickly shuts the lid, before the smoke can escape.

"What is that, Titi?"

"¿El calderón? Es from family of your great-grandfather."

I also wonder what a coincidence it is that Mami's maiden name also means cauldron. Is brujería in our blood?

"I know that's what it means, Titi, but I want to know what's *in* the pot right there."

"No, es true. Es gift from my father. He give to me. He had el aché too."

Was this some sort of family legacy to evade direct questions? I am starting to get annoyed when she adds . . .

"Oye, m'ijita, when time is right, I will tell you all I know. Te prometo."

Thank goodness she doesn't say "when you're older," because if one more adult says this to me I just know I'll start screaming. But Yaya doesn't seem like most adults, and she promised me, so I'll let this one slide.

"OK, Titi." And then I say the words that I am reluctant to say. "I gotta go."

"Sí. I know. Pero primero . . ."

She opens the cauldron with one hand and grabs the güiro with the other. Then she takes a wooden spoon and ladles out the somewhat chunky concoction into it. I watch as she puts the top half of the güiro onto the bottom half to seal it, wraps the whole thing in plastic wrap, places it in a paper sack, and extends her arm toward me.

"Toma. Take it." She puts the small paper bag in my hand, like she is sending me to school with my lunch.

"What's in it?" I ask.

"No te preocupes. This will help you. Keep it near your window for seven days, to give it light. Then bring it back to me."

"OK, Titi. Gracias." I want to ask her, *Help me with what?* But I doubt I'll get my answer today. Besides, I'm running out of time.

I put one hand on the bottom of the bag and one hand on top to secure its contents and begin my exit.

"De nada, Maya. You've made a viejita's day." She puts her hands on my shoulders.

"¿El azabache? ¿Te sirve bien?"

Wait. Did she give it to me? I mean, how else would she know? "Uh huh. The azabache has served me well so far," I answer. I don't have the heart to tell her I already lost it.

"Bueno. Keep wearing it," she says.

"How did you . . . How did I . . . get it?"

"My aché. Your aché. Can do magical things together. To have the aché is a gift—a gift you share with the world. I share mine with you."

∼ ∼ ∼

I want to squeal with delight as I leave the apartment holding the paper bag carefully in my hands. I feel like hopping on the 6 train and shouting from atop the Empire State Building:

"Titi Yaya is for real!! And she picked MEEEEEEE!!!!"

Wait. I shouldn't get too geeked over this. What about this orisha, Yemaya? The rational, Papi-part of me would say this is preposterous. God doesn't exist, remember? But he is the one who told me about all these deities from West Africa that pre-date modern religion. Mami and Abuela, the Christians they are, would say this is false idolatry. But this feels different. This feels like destiny.

Chapter 16
Sister Problems

BEFORE I LEFT Titi Yaya's apartment, I checked the clock: 10:12 p.m., which means I've been gone for twenty-eight minutes. This is cutting it close. Instead of going back down the stairs that lead directly into the kitchen, I use the staircase that leads to the main door of the apartment building, around the corner, to make it look like I had been on a delivery. At this time, Tio Fausto is normally closing the back of the house. Mami will be with him, wrapping up in the kitchen. Abuela and Abuelo will have already headed home to bed. Titi Julia will be at home minding Ini, Mini, and Mo. Trini is probably still flirting with Jam—OH MY GOD!

I turn and bump right into the canoodling couple as they are hugging up on each other around the corner of the building. Trini looks at me and panics.

She pushes Jamal away and pleads, "Don't tell Fausto! He'll kill us both!"

Jamal clears his throat, trying not to look embarrassed in front of his former patient. "So, uh, I take it you're feeling better, Maya?" he stammers.

I open my mouth to answer, but then Trini interrupts. "Heeeey, what are you doing out here anyway? Did you sneak off to visit Titi Yaya or something?"

Before I start to panic myself, I realize that I have the upper hand, so I don't have to answer her. Trini has just as much to lose as I do. I simply say, "Look, I won't tell if you won't tell."

"Deal," Trini says, a little too desperately.

I turn the corner and make my way inside the restaurant from the street entrance And now, the only person really standing in my way would be . . .

Salma! ¡Carajo!

There she is, right in front of me, like she was waiting this whole time. Stone-cold busted in the doorway. She is most definitely in her viejita mode, holding a broom, and tapping her foot like an old lady.

Salma tips her glasses up her nose to get a closer look at me. "Where have you been, Maya? Mami's worried that you got jumped or something making a delivery."

"Nah, Sal, todo tranquilo," I say, trying to play it cool. I shift my weight onto my left leg to appear casual. "I, um, made a delivery to Señora Infante's place, and you know how she is! She, um, cornered me, and you know, of course, she had to offer me some dessert. And, you know, it was a slice of tres leches cake, so you know, I couldn't resist."

I can't believe I'm making the señora an accessory to my crime. But I'm sure she'd understand, under the circumstances.

"Rosario Infante ordered takeout? That's hard to believe," Salma states, like the junior tormentor she is.

"Why? She loves our food," I say, pushing past her, thinking that if I keep playing it cool, she'll back off. But she doesn't fall for it, and walks behind me.

"No, I mean, if she wanted something to eat, why didn't she just come in?"

"I don't know Salma! Maybe she was too tired to walk over! Geez, why do you ask such silly questions? You on Mami's payroll or something?"

She zeros in on the paper sack in my hand. "So, what's in the bag?"

"Leftover tres leches cake. And don't ask me for none cuz it's mine!" I say quickly, grabbing the bag tighter.

"Well, you look guilty, Maya. Unless you were making out with Nestor Garcia in the back alley . . . I'd say you were upstairs with Yaya!"

I turn around at that accusation. "What is this? A game of *Clue*? Look, I wouldn't be caught dead making out with Nestor . . ."

"Aha! So, you *were* upstairs!" She points a finger in my face like a smug detective solving a crime.

"I didn't say that . . ."

"I knew it! I knew it! That paper bag gave you away! Just like Trini said, all the others left Titi Yaya's apartment with one," she finishes, pleased at herself. "Plus, I overheard Abuela carrying on earlier about how upset you made her, getting in her business, wearing that stone around your neck like you're some kind of bruja in training . . ."

"Stop it, Sal! Stop it! I don't want to hear any more of this!" I can't think of any more excuses because my sister has me pegged.

"What do you want, Maya? Are you trying to get in trouble? Do you want to be another black sheep in the family? Cuz all I have to do is tell Mami and it'll all be over for you . . ." She points to the kitchen for emphasis.

"Please, Salma, don't!" My voice is desperate now. But I am in no position to bargain.

Salma shakes the broomstick at me. "Y'know, I'm sick and tired of you being the Golden Child. Give me one good reason why I shouldn't . . ."

"You're just jelly that Yaya didn't pick you!" I cross my arms in defiance.

"Ha! Pick me for what? To become a witch's apprentice? Why would I care?" She shakes the broomstick at me again. "Maybe you should just take this broom and fly, fly away, brujita . . ."

"Ay, Salchicha! I can't believe you would buy into that basura . . ." I wave my free hand at her to get her out of my face.

She just stands there, one hand on her hip, dripping with disdain. It's obvious I am not gonna change her mind for nothing.

I throw up my right hand, careful not to tip the gourd inside the bag I'm holding with my left. "Y'know what? Do what you want. I'm outta here."

I breeze by her again, hoping that my indifference will turn her off from being the snitch.

"Okaaaaay, I won't tell," she calls after me.

I spin around and cock my head to the side in surprise. "What'd you say?"

"I said I won't tell. But . . ."

I know when dealing with Salchicha there's bound to be a big butt sticking out somewhere.

"But what?"

She pauses to contemplate my sentence. "You gotta do my chores for a month."

"A month?!? C'mon! You can't play prosecutor, jury, and judge at the same time!" I protest. Salma really could follow in Papi's footsteps as a lawyer if she wanted to.

"Or . . . I tell, and you could be grounded—who knows? Mami might be so heated that you deliberately disobeyed the family, she might sentence you for longer. No soccer, no internet, no instant messaging prima Taina or your little girlfriend Kayla or . . ."

"Stop it! Stop! No way. Two weeks." Why I think I can negotiate these terms I'll never know.

"Three weeks." She crosses her arms and stands her ground.

"Alright. Done." I extend my right hand.

"Deal." Salma takes my hand and seals the deal.

"Pues, vamos. Let's check in with Mami in the kitchen," I say.

"Yeah, before she comes out and busts us both," Salma laughs. And then, after a beat, she adds softly: "We really were worried."

Hmmm, maybe I'm wrong about my hermanita. Sure, I got a raw deal, but it could have been worse. This is an act of—dare I say—mercy.

And doing extra chores for three weeks seems like a small price to pay for a sliver of forbidden freedom.

Chapter 17

Who Is Yemaya?

As a reward for working hard on Friday night, Tio Fausto gives us kids a break from the brunch shift on Saturday. That means sleeping in—but it still doesn't excuse us from doing housework—and I now have Salma's chores to worry about too. When I wake up, it's raining, which means the soccer match will be postponed till tomorrow, so I don't have anywhere to be this afternoon. So, I decide to do a little internet research. Not for school (I'll get to that later), but I want to look up things based on what Yaya had told me.

So, I am the daughter of Yemaya. Who is she? Luckily, this is easier information to unearth on the internet than the meaning of aché. Turns out there's a whole pantheon of gods and goddesses in what's called the Regla Lucumí. Funny, we learn all about Greek and Roman mythology in school, but nothing about Yoruba deities—just like Papi told me on the phone. History teachers also talk about slavery in the United States and the colonies, but not in the Caribbean, where slavery started more than one hundred years earlier.

Once the Spanish conquistadores left their bloody mark by forcing the Taíno and West Africans to choose between Catholicism or death, these people adapted to practice their Yoruba religion in secret. For centuries, there have been people from the islands to mainland Africa who have been determined to keep the ancient traditions alive. Titi Yaya is one of them. And now she wants to pass down these traditions onto me. How can anyone be mad at that?

I continue reading. Yemaya is known as La Diosa del Mar, Goddess of the Sea, the mother of all life and protector of women and children. In Africa, she is known as Mama Watta, as in Mother of the Waves. Yemaya is also sometimes referred to as La Sirena—the mermaid. Her number is seven, as in the Seven Seas. Her name is a contraction of Yey Omo Eja, which means, "Mother of the children who are fish."

I was born on March seventh. Day seven. And I'm a Pisces. The sign of the fish. Huh.

I toggle to Google image search and see breathtaking drawings and paintings of Yemaya on my computer screen. The orisha is represented reverently with dark skin and flowing black hair, dressed in various hues of marine blue and aqua—and in some depictions, she's shown as a mermaid. I look around my room with fresh eyes. There has to be other logical explanations for blue being my favorite color, for liking mermaids, for feeling a connection to the ocean, and for being a Pisces born on the seventh day of March. But at that moment, I can't think of any. Are these all signs that I've been a child of Yemaya all this time? If so, that's pretty dope.

There's a whole pantheon to learn about and I'm just scratching the surface. I'm hoping Titi Yaya will teach me more about these gods and goddesses. Little do I realize how much I am going to learn . . .

Chapter 18

Another Visitor

INSTEAD OF YEMAYA who comes into my dream that night, it is another orisha. And it feels more like a nightmare . . .

I am back on the beach. Thunder, lightning, and wind threaten me as I stand on the shoreline, whipping my hair every which way. I am having trouble standing up.

"Jekua Jey Yansá Oya!" I hear the voice rise above the storm as the orisha announces herself. Even though I don't understand the language, I somehow deduce that she is announcing her presence. Oya's voice doesn't sound anything like Yemaya's soothing tone. It is deeper, more forceful, and commanding.

Draped in a flowy gown the color of red wine (or is it dried blood?), Oya approaches me, floating down from the sky while carrying a flaming torch in one hand, a sword in another. Her long, black hair is undulating in the wind.

She has on a metal headdress, like she is going to battle. Her face is hidden, but I feel her gaze as her fiery eyes bear into me. She alternates swinging the torch and the sword above and around her head, forming bolts of lightning in the sky, which grows darker with each passing moment.

I stand there, frozen. The sand feels like cement burying my feet.

"No tengas miedo," the gruff voice of Oya calls as I try to regain my balance.

How can I not be afraid? Kind of hard not to, with a masked woman in blood red coming at me with a blade and fire and all.

I manage to eke out, "What do you want?"

"El cambio viene," she says.

The winds blow around me like a personal tornado and keep repeating this phrase. Change is coming. That's it. *El cambio viene.*

When I shoot up out of bed, I realize I am out of breath and my heart is racing. I grab the thermos that sits bedside and take a big gulp of water.

I feel like worlds are colliding, and that I'm caught between reality and an overwhelming ethereal energy. Change is as inevitable as the tides coming in. And there is nothing I can do about it. But what have I gotten myself mixed up in?

The orisha told me not to be afraid. How can I not freak out, though, after a nightmare like that? I take another sip from my water bottle to take me down a notch, so I can think.

So, Oya brings the winds of change. Is that good or bad? Either way, change is headed my way—or it's already here, and I have to deal with it. Whether it's the neighborhood I've spent my whole life in becoming unrecognizable, or these new feelings I have for Kayla, I'm realizing that change can be external or internal. Certainly, the sudden arrival of Titi Yaya has sent this family into a tizzy—and it has unearthed family secrets and emotions that have been long buried. Can the relationship between my Abuela and Titi Yaya be mended? Can I help change that? Or am I making things worse by befriending her? I seem to have a special connection to my great aunt, my Yoruba roots, and an ancient religion. But what if my family finds out and decides to kick me to the curb too? They've done it before—so that means they could do it again, right? That would be too much to bear. Or an even worse fate . . . what if this change means that someone might get sick . . . or even die? My family means everything to me. I need to calm down.

Chapter 19

Meanwhile, Back at the Café...

SUNDAY MORNING, I wake up still rattled from Oya's surprise appearance in my dream. Then my heart sinks when I remember that my soccer match is happening this afternoon, without me.

I walk over to the semi-clean pile of clothes and throw on a pair of black leggings and a baby blue tee with the word CHULA bedazzled in hot pink and head over to Café Taza.

At 9:30a.m., it's still a little too early for the brunch rush (New Yorkers like to eat late on weekends). So there are just a trio of regular coffee drinkers at the counter, including Aracely from the Dominican hair salon, who is carrying her daughter Kiara, or Kiki, on her hip. She's

Trini's stylist, and right now she is trying to convince my titi to dye her hair Rihanna Red.

"Te lo digo, nena, that color would look so fuego on you!" Aracely tells Trini while shifting her weight to accommodate her growing toddler. I look at Kiara's chubby arm go up as she curiously reaches for her mami's coffee cup. Is that an azabache tied around her wrist? These ancient traditions sure do travel far across the generations.

"I dunno . . . I feel like Fausto might freak out," Trini says.

"You do everything your big brother says? You are an independent woman!" Aracely bursts out, practically daring her into making the transformation before interrupting herself. "Kiara, no!" She bats her toddler's hand away and picks up the coffee cup. (I feel you, Kiki.)

"I'll think about it," Trini says wistfully.

Meanwhile, Salma, Ini, Mini, and Mo are seated at our regular back booth and helping themselves from a large stack of pancakes that Trini has just plopped in front of them, before heading back into the kitchen.

"Ayo, savages! Save some for me!" I say, as I make Salma scooch over.

I give her thigh an extra pat—y'know, a gesture of nonchalant sisterly love for not totally busting me last night. She smiles before popping a tiered, syrupy bite of pancake into her mouth. I look around for something to drink. Ever since Señora Infante started giving me the leche con café, I've sort of been craving it. Uh-oh, am I turning into a coffee drinker now? This might be a problem. I settle on pouring myself a glass of orange juice from the pitcher, take a sip, and am left with an unsatisfied tang in my mouth. It's nowhere near the same. (Caffeine>>>Sugar)

Trini comes back from the kitchen with an appetizer plate of scrambled eggs y nada más and stands behind the counter.

"I'm trying to watch my carbs," she says sadly, looking at her pitiful plate.

"Good luck with that," I say. Puerto Rican diets are built around starches: Rice! Beans! Bread! Yuca! Potatoes! Corn!

"Yeah, that just means more panqueques for us!" Ini says while Mini clinks forks with her twin sister.

But Trini has one advantage over us: she is old enough for café con leche—and the aroma coming from her cup is torturing me.

"So, even after that big mess last night, Jamal asked me out. Can you believe it? Me? Dating a doctor?" Trini takes a sip of coffee.

"He's not a doctor *yet*," Salma reminds her.

"I know, pero *still* . . ." she swoons.

"Y'know, Tio Fausto's gonna lose it one of these days if you don't stop flirting with the customers. You want him to get arrested protecting his hermanita?" I say.

"I guess you're right." Trini wants to be grown so bad, but right now she's pouting like a little girl. "But Jamal is special." She twirls a forkful of eggs in the air, before taking a bite.

Just then, Tio Fausto walks by with a rack of silverware, plops it down on the counter with force, and bellows, "Damn right, Trini. Mira, I can't have you flirting with the customers!"

"Technically, I flirted with Jamal at the hospital first, so it doesn't count," Trini answers defiantly.

All of us girls chuckle at the exchange. Mo is clueless, but Fausto is not amused. "¡Basta ya! I'm gonna have you stop working the weekend night shifts. I don't need the agita."

"Ay, Fausto, pero I need those tips. That's my college money you're messing with!" Trini protests.

"Well, maybe if you focused more on your studies than boys, you could have earned a scholarship!" Fausto snaps back. Dang.

Trini's whole face falls. Big brothers have a way of cutting to the bone, and that was a low blow. She looks down, stands up, and without another word, takes her plate of now cold eggs back to the kitchen.

Pobrecita Trini. She is a crazy-talented artist, but people only seem to judge her based on her looks. She has learned how to use her beauty to her advantage, but it must feel hollow and lonely at times. Being the baby sister doesn't help either. Tio Fausto is so overprotective and so old school. Standing there in the silence, he makes a gesture like he is going follow Trini to the kitchen, but then instead mumbles something about having to greet Table Four.

PFFFZZZZZTTTTTT! Mo breaks the uncomfortable silence—and my train of thought—by breaking wind.

"Excuse me," he squeaks.

"Oh, c'mon, Mo!! We're eating over here!" Then we all bust out into laughter. Nothing like a fart to ease the tension.

After the giggle fit dies down, who should roll up but Kayla and her mom. Kayla's hair is braided into an elaborate pattern of cornrows today. It makes her almond-shaped eyes look even bigger and more soulful and her face more angular. She is a taller and more athletic version of her mom, and they share the same bright smile.

"Hey girl, whassup?" she says.

"Nada mucho." *Keep cool, Maya.* I look around nervously, hoping Mo's stink bomb isn't still lingering. "You here for brunch?"

"Yeah, girl. I heard about how fire your huevos rancheros are. I figured I'd fill up before the big g—oh, sorry, Maya."

"Hey, it's cool," I say, trying not to look disappointed. "Hopefully, I can leave work early and come cheer you guys on. Anyway, I'm glad you came. Hi, Kayla's mom."

"Hi, Maya," Ms. Phillips greets me. "I forgot how nice this place is. Sorry we haven't been back sooner."

I know they've been on a serious budget. When Kayla's dad left them a couple years ago, she transferred to our middle school. She and her mom have been going through it ever since—food stamps, unemployment, temporary homelessness, the works. New York City can be harsh sometimes—and sometimes, it swallows people whole. But you'd never know they were having a hard time just by looking at them. Not only do they have a positive attitude, but Kayla must've inherited her mom's style on a dime—putting together fly outfits with unique pieces she finds at thrift stores. "Girl, this vest cost me two dollars!" Kayla will brag. Today, she's just wearing her uniform, of course, but she wears it well.

I think about asking Tio Fausto if he could comp their meal. Maybe he wouldn't be such a notorious cheapskate today. On second thought . . . naaahhhhh. He'll always be a cheapskate. I'll figure something out on my own.

"Come sit," I say as I guide them to a booth. Already, Fausto would chastise me for seating a party of two at a four-top. But I don't care.

"May I start you off with a café con leche?" I start in my grandiose hostess-with-the-mostest way, which, for some reason, consists of a fake British accent.

"Yes, make it two."

"Excelente. I'll make them myself!" I exclaim. That way, I won't have to put the coffees on the final tab. I also manage to order an extra huevos rancheros for them so that it won't show up in the receipt system—that way, they'll only have to pay for one dish.

At the end of the meal, they've eaten like queens on a BOGO deal. I feel good about taking care of my friend and her mom. They didn't have to come see me, and yet, here they are.

Just as I drop the check on the table and thank them for coming, the salsa music turns up. There's something intoxicating about the syncopated beat of Latin music when the clave hits on the two and the three, then again on the five, six, and seven—an infectious beat that always gets toes tapping, hips swaying, and hands clapping. Salsa magic.

Abuelo Chucho comes shimmying through the aisles, looking dapper in his butter yellow guayabera, searching for a dance partner. He sets his sights on Kayla's mom and smoothes what's left of his frizzy hair down.

"Señora, may I have this dance?" Abuelo asks gallantly.

"Of course!" She extends her hand and lets him whisk her away as the trumpets kick in to pepper the track.

When our giggles settle down, Kayla says to me, "Yo, your family is something."

"I told you they were a wild bunch. Let's just hope my Abuela doesn't get jealous of your mom. She's very pretty—like you."

Kayla smiles. "Thank you. You are too. In fact, your whole family is good looking. It's kinda sickening, actually. And they all seem so nice."

Now it's my turn to smile and blush. But maybe if she knew how our family has banished one of their own, she wouldn't think that way. I wish I could tell her about Titi Yaya, staying just right above us, and the mysterious gourd that she gave me that's now sitting on my windowsill. But I figure Kayla has enough to deal with than to be bogged down by my family problems.

Instead, I blurt out, "I like your braids."

"Oh, thanks, my auntie hooked me up," she says, touching her head. "It's so much easier to deal with my hair when it's back and off my face when I'm playing soccer."

"Speaking of which, doesn't the game start soon?" I ask.

"Ohmigosh, you're right! Ma! We gotta go!" she calls over the music. Ms. Phillips walks back to the booth to gather her purse. Abuelo looks disappointed by the loss of his dance partner. So am I, actually. I wish Kayla could stay. Or better yet, that I could play in the game with her. Any reason to spend more time with her.

"You're not coming to the game?" Kayla asks. She looks genuinely disappointed and I am touched.

"My mom won't let me go until after the second half. She doesn't trust that I won't try to play."

Kayla laughs. "Well, knowing how you are, she's probably got a point. I'll see you in the second half then?"

"Yeah. See you then," I say, trying not to look disappointed myself.

I watch her jog away, then I plop down in the booth in double defeat.

Before I can get too down on myself, Kayla comes running back to me—and plants a quick peck on my cheek. "Thanks again for everything," she says. And after making quick eye contact with me, she darts back outside.

I grin from ear to ear. I like someone and she likes me! It's not my imagination! The feelings are actually mutual! I'm not quite sure what I'm supposed to do next, but let me just relish this moment . . .

"Maya! Get up and clean that table off! I need to seat a party of three!"

Leave it to Tio Fausto to disturb my groove.

Chapter 20
Titi Sister Cousin

WHEN THE BRUNCH RUSH is over, it's time for the family to eat—sandwiches cubanos for everyone, with shredded roast pernil (pork shoulder), sliced ham, Swiss cheese, pickles, and mustard on toasted baguettes, fresh from Señora Infante's bakery. Mami includes a side of fresh fruit for each of us instead of papas fritas, to make sure we get our daily dose of fiber. We eat so well it's not even funny. Trini reluctantly picks the ham out of the bread and starts nibbling on the meat.

After I finish half of my sandwich, Mami say it's OK to take the rest to-go so I can check out the soccer game, as long as Trini chaperones. We both groan at first, but y'know, it's rare that I get to spend any time alone with my young aunt. She usually has so much going on juggling design school and work, plus my other cousins are always around. I have to admire her hustle. After a block or two of silence, I start up a conversation while I finish my cubano.

"Y'know, I don't really think Tio Fausto is going to cut your hours. He needs you too much," I say, hoping to console her.

"Oh, I know. My big brother is all bluster. He just loses his mind when he sees a man around me. I'll never get a boyfriend this way. Maybe that's his mission," Trini says.

"Hey, there's always Oscar," I say, knowing this will get a reaction.

"Yeah, good ol' Oscar," she replies before heaving a big sigh. "Mira, the way I feel about Oscar is exactly how you feel about Nestor."

I roll my eyes. "OK, OK. I totally get it," I say.

Trini continues, "Oscar's sweet and all, but I want something more than literally just the guy next door. I want someone to expand my horizons, to encourage me to reach my true potential, to see me for who I am. Don't you want out of this barrio one day?"

"I dunno. What's wrong with it?" I've never known anything else than Brooklyn.

"Girl, even just going to school in Manhattan has opened my eyes to the possibilities. There's more to life than just our little restaurant, Jorge's bodega, and Infante Bakery. I mean, think about it. Dolores got out and is now living a glamourous life in LA."

"Yeah, I guess you're right." I do think about it for a minute, wondering what my own future holds. Will I be a soccer star and earn a scholarship to college somewhere? Or will I become a curandera like Titi Yaya? New ways, versus the old ways. ¿Por qué no los dos?

Then I add, "What about Jamal? You two looked pretty close last night. That could be a possibility."

Trini's face lights up. "Yeah, I think it could be too. So, thanks for not telling Fausto about seeing us. Cuz I really like Jamal and I don't want him messing it up for me. Jamal is taking me to the Metropolitan Museum of Art later this week so we can see the Costume Institute. He thinks it might inspire me at school."

"That's actually pretty cool," I say.

"See? That's the kind of stuff I'm looking for. The designer and the doctor—has a nice ring to it, doesn't it?"

"Yeah, it kinda does. I hope it works out," I say in earnest.

As we enter the park, which means getting closer to seeing Kayla, I realize I can use some love advice of my own.

"Say, Trini, can I ask you a question?"

"Yes?" Her big brown eyes get even bigger with curiosity.

"How do you know when someone's into you?" I am suddenly bashful.

A cat-like grin takes over Trini's face. This is her sweet spot. "Ohhh, there are lots of ways. But I'll tell you this: If they come to your restaurant to see you, that's usually a pretty big sign."

I pause from taking a bite of my sandwich. "Heeeeyyyy, are you talking about you or me?"

Trini stops walking, turns around to face me, and gives me a knowing look. "Well, both of us, really. Nena, I saw your friend Kayla at the café. The same one from the Wonder Wheel, right? Girl, she's way into you. The question now becomes . . . are you into her?"

Am I really going to admit that I have a crush on a girl to my Titi Trini? I can't imagine talking to Mami or Papi about this right now. Salma? No way. Pero it's a feeling I've had for a while, that I just can't shake. I gotta fess up.

"You won't tell anyone?" I plead.

"Not until you're ready, Maya. I promise." She crosses her heart to reassure me.

"OK then . . ." I take a deep breath before I continue, "I *am* into her. I just don't know what to do about it."

"Eeee! I knew it! I can always sense a budding romance!" Trini squeals and does a little twirl of joy.

"OK, OK . . . Chill!" I let out a nervous laugh, realizing we're almost there. "So, what do I do about it?"

"Just tell her!" Trini says excitedly. "And y'know, just let it flow from there."

"I think I can do that," I say, not quite confidently. But I'm hoping the courage will come to me once I'm in the moment.

"Good. Now let me have a bite of that sandwich." Trini reaches for my hand like that greedy toddler Kiki.

I extend my arm so the sandwich is out of her reach. "Wait! I thought you were on a diet!"

"Yeah, and it's killing me," she says while swiping the sandwich from my hand. She takes a huge bite and moans. "Carajo, whatever Rosario Infante does to her bread just isn't fair," she adds with her mouth full.

That makes me wonder if Señora Infante really does sprinkle a little magic in her flour? Maybe Titi Yaya gives her a special salsa in her brown paper bag or something.

"You can have the rest. I won't tell," I say. I love that Trini and I are suddenly bonding over keeping each other's secrets.

WHEN WE ARRIVE at the soccer field, Kayla is making an offensive move, running up the right side of the field. Lissette, who took my place playing the CAM—kicks the ball ahead of Kayla, who times her footsteps perfectly to get to the penalty box just as the goalie creeps out. Before the defenders can catch up to her, Kayla plants her right foot, swings her left foot back, and follows through with her instep. The ball sails and hits the crossbar and then ricochets into the net. GOAL!!! The Warriors then rally to wind down the clock until the ref blows the whistle. Winning 1–0 is enough to get us into the championship—YAY!—where we'll be playing the Honey Badgers again. Boooo!

Trini hangs out a few feet away from the sidelines as both teams line up to say "good game" and pass around high fives. I rush over to my team to join the celebration. When Kayla sees me, her flushed, sweaty face beams.

"Did you see the goal?" she asks with excitement.

"I did! We arrived just in time. You sure love to hit that crossbar," I smile.

"Eh, it's working for me," she says with a shrug. "Still, it wasn't the same without you."

We share a look. "Aww, thanks. Believe me, I would've much rather been playing soccer with y'all than bussing tables."

"Yeah, like I said before, we make a good team." There goes that double entendre again.

There's an awkward silence between us, but it's lost on all my teammates, who are still riding high on victory.

I decide to wait until the herd thins out before I take it one step further. Trini is buying me time by flirting with Coach, but she keeps giving me looks of encouragement over his shoulder. I tell her to chill with my eyes.

A few minutes later, Kayla seems to sense the opportunity at just the right time. It is pretty much just the two of now, with just a couple of stragglers.

"Thanks again for brunch this afternoon," she says.

"You're welcome. Thanks for coming." It's now or never. "So, uhhhhh . . . about earlier . . ." I start.

"Yeah, about that. You mad?" She starts aimlessly kicking divots in the grass.

"No!" I say a little too quickly, before reminding myself to chill. "No way. I liked it." I pause and then take my voice lower, before saying, "I like . . . you."

She looks up and straight into my eyes. "You do? Good. I like you too."

We both smile and giggle.

"So . . . now what?" I ask cautiously.

Kayla shrugs. "I don't know. I've never done this before."

"Me either. I guess we just go with the flow," I say, echoing Trini's words of advice.

"So, hug it out, I guess?" she asks, while opening up her arms.

"Hug it out." And I fall inside her embrace.

It's the warmest, sweetest hug I've ever shared with someone not related to me. It probably lingers a little too long for just two teammates. But at this moment, I don't care.

ON THE WAY HOME, walking back through the park, I give Trini a sideways hug.

"See? Now we are both crushing on someone who likes us back. Feels good, doesn't it?" Trini reassures me.

"It sure does. Now I get why you are such a romantic," I respond.

Trini laughs mellifluously. I realize I've missed this part of our relationship. Sure, she's my aunt—but she has always been more of a sister-cousin. On days like today, I'm glad I have her.

Just then, a piragüero pushes his cart by us on the sidewalk. MMmmmm—shaved ice with deliciously Caribbean-flavored syrup scooped into a paper cup. Fat free—but definitely not carb-friendly. Before I can even ask . . .

"Want a piragua?" Trini asks me, her eyes wide.

I am surprised by the offer. "What about your diet?"

"What diet?" she says mischievously.

We both bust out laughing.

"Sure. Coco for me," I say.

Trini flags the piragüero down and orders a large coconut for me, and a small pineapple for her. We walk over to a nearby bench to slurp them up. No sense in letting the ice and sticky syrup melt all over us while we walk. Plus, I want to savor every moment of everything that has happened to me today.

Trini is obviously in a genial and generous mood, so I decide to ask her a little bit more about my family. Maybe she can connect some more dots for me.

"Trini, do you feel close with your sisters? With my mom and Titi Dolores?" I take a lick of my coconutty icy treat.

"Define close," she says matter-of-factly, as she navigates her cup. "Soledad and Dolores are both a lot older than me and one moved three thousand miles away."

"That's what I thought. But I guess I just feel like I know so little about them. Even about my own mom. I'm just wondering if they have any connection to Titi Yaya . . . you know, like I have with you."

"I don't know. I do know that Titi Yaya used to take care of Soledad and Dolores until they were like, ten and eleven, while my folks were on the road. But neither my mom nor your mom speaks of it. I think that's when the rift began. Because Fausto and I have never been allowed to know our tía."

"That's so messed up," I say.

We watch a young couple walk by with some kind of poodle hybrid on a leash. People are mixing poodles with any ol' breed to make them so they don't shed. It's like some mad science experiment.

"I know. I feel like my sisters went through a lot when they were little, like before I was born. Mom and Dad were always traveling in their dance career, and they stopped traveling after having Fausto. I was the 'oops' baby, after they retired from dancing, so I never experienced that feeling of missing my parents for long periods of time like they did. I'm sure it was hard on my sisters. But neither of them really talks about it. Plus, for whatever it's worth, their names mean loneliness and pain. It's kinda hard to relate to that."

"Wow," I say. "I just can't imagine not talking to Salma for twenty years, or not being able to speak to my aunt who took care of me. Can you?" A light September breeze blows through our hair, giving us a break from the afternoon sun.

"No, I can't. But that's a different generation. They are more set in their ways, slow to forgive, and they bottle things up. It's really not healthy. Sometimes, it's up to the younger generation to jumpstart the healing process. So, I think it's a good thing that you're hanging out with Titi Yaya, Maya. She doesn't seem so bad." She smiles in tacit approval.

I take my last few licks of my piragua and crush my paper cup. "Yeah, she's actually pretty wonderful," I reply. "That would be great if she could be part of the family again."

"Well, if anyone can do it, you can." Trini smiles at me, then takes one last spoonful and crushes her cup too—which is part of the piragua ritual.

"Thanks, Trini. For everything." I put my arm around her and rest my head on her shoulder.

"No problem." She leans her head over mine and we stay like that for a good thirty seconds. Then her phone buzzes. She looks at the screen and groans. "Ugh, Fausto is texting me to make sure I'm back by the dinner shift. Duh, bro."

"Like I said, he needs you too much," I remind her.

"Pues, vámonos, muchacha."

We get up from the bench and make our way back to the café.

Chapter 21
Balance & Blessings

THE NEXT FIVE DAYS are sort of a blur—a mix of excitement and wonderment. Part of me is anxiously counting down until Friday, when Titi Yaya told me to come back. I can hardly wait to see what she has in store for me with that gourd filled with mysterious herbs. How I manage to keep everyone from noticing a janky-looking vessel in my windowsill for almost a week, I'll never know.

But the other part of me is too busy swooning over taking this friendship with Kayla to the next level. Starting on Monday, she meets me in front of the school as me and la ganga roll up. After my sister and my cousins disperse, we share my leche con café (Señora Infante keeps on hooking me up) and I give her half my roll with jam.

At lunch, we blend in with the rest of the soccer girls at our usual table, but there is a hidden spark between us as we exchange furtive glances at one another. I happily supplement her boring school meal with some of the deliciousness that Mami packed that morning. Because for Latines, food means love. On Thursday, we exchange homemade bracelets. I am on Cloud Nine.

FRIDAY MORNING, I wake up wondering how everything is going to come together. Will smoke suddenly start rising and sparks come flying out of this gourd? Nope, nada . . . at least for now. Though it does smell a little funky.

As I get dressed, I hear a low buzzing sound outside my window. It isn't like the normal noise that Brooklyn makes in the morning with its burping traffic and— lately—loud construction, as the neighborhood gets reshaped brownstone by brownstone. It sounds too . . . beautiful. Mesmerizing, even. I reach over to the curtains and pull them to the side, and there I see an emerald green hummingbird on the other side of the glass, well, humming. Instead of looking for a flower, the bird seems to be looking at—well, me.

"Dude, like, how often are hummingbirds just chillin' in Nueva York?" I ask no one as I turn to the mirror and start to fuss with my hair, which is being particularly unruly today. I pick up the water bottle from the dresser and start spritzing my curls into submission.

But the hummingbird continues to hover in front of my bedroom window, as if it is trying to get my attention. I put the spray bottle down and inch closer to the window, extending my index finger on the glass. The hummingbird, its wings just a whirling blur, puts its slender beak up to match my finger on the other side. It then makes a loop-de-loop up in the sky then dives right back to the same spot in front of my window. This dance lasts for a few minutes, and then, suddenly, the hummingbird is gone.

I scratch my damp head and look up to the clouds, where the hummingbird seemed to be headed. Then I realize the hummingbird's feathers are the same color as Titi Yaya's eyes. She is calling me. And I am compelled to obey—even if it means disobeying the rest of the adults in my family. After all, Titi Yaya is my family too.

I peek inside the gourd. The contents have dried up, into almost like a powder. Salsa magic strikes again. I go downstairs to grab some plastic wrap from the kitchen and bring it back up to cover the gourd, to keep whatever is inside from spilling out, and put it gently at the bottom of my messenger bag. I decide I will sneak up to Titi Yaya's after school, while my sister and my cousins have their afternoon snack at the café.

AT LUNCH TIME, I'm not really interested in what my soccer teammates will have to say. My mind is elsewhere. I want to talk to Kayla about my secret so bad. I need to get it off my chest. Kayla walks into the cafeteria. She has denim jeans on that are cut off at the thigh, and she is wearing a men's oxford shirt paired with a striped sweater vest that looks like a grandpa could've owned it. But as usual, she makes it work. I pull her aside and say, "I have something to tell you." I lead her to an empty table in the corner.

"I'm all ears," she says eagerly, and then sits down.

I sit opposite Kayla and lean in. "OK, so I have this secret great aunt who lives above the restaurant who I'm never allowed to visit," I start, realizing that sentence must sound unhinged to any normal person. But it's too late to take it back now.

Kayla's eyes widen. "That's so weird. Your family seems too nice to keep secrets like that," she says.

"That's what I thought. But apparently, it's a long-standing beef between my Abuela and her sister from Puerto Rico, who just rolled into town out of the blue last week."

"Oh wow, this is some real drama!" Kayla exclaims, still in awe.

"But here's the crazy part: This woman has been coming to me in my dreams for like, months and months already!

"Girl, get out!" she says in an excited whisper.

"Yeah, it's been so weird. So, one day, I decided to sneak upstairs and meet her face to face. And it was like I already knew her! Turns out she's this amazing curandera—a mystical healer—and she picked me to carry on our Yoruba traditions!"

Kayla's mouth drops open. "Maya, that is *wild*! What are you going to do?"

"Well, I'm going to sneak up there again after school today to get more details—because there's still so much I don't know."

Kayla purses her lips before speaking now. "Maya, be careful. You can't keep sneaking around your family. You'll get caught eventually and then you'll get in trouble!"

"I know, I know. But I don't know what else to do!" I respond.

"Just promise me this will be the last time. Hopefully, you'll get the answers you need. But I think your family has to squash this beef first before you can go on. You can't be caught in the middle. I know how much your family means to you."

She is absolutely right. "OK, I promise. Just wish me luck," I say.

"Good luck, Maya." With a concerned smile, she reaches across the table and puts her hand on top of mine. It feels good to finally tell her the truth. And hey, she didn't run away after all!

It's NOT EASY to convince anyone in my family that you have no appetite, but I will sure have to try. Latines are food pushers, and will try to get you to eat a little some-thing even if you're not in the mood. Trini always goes with "cramps," and since I just started getting my period a few months ago, I have learned that menstrual cramps are no joke. So, I clutch my abdomen and try that excuse on for size. Salma shoots me a quick side eye, yet no one else seems to notice that I'm faking. I walk away doubled over with my messenger bag in hand.

I pretend to go home, but instead, I detour through the apartment building entrance around the corner. I buzz Titi Yaya's apartment and hear the main door click open. When I go upstairs, I see her front door open a crack, a signal for me to walk in.

"Quítate los zapatos," she says in her deep but sooth-ing voice. I take off my shoes and I grab the gourd out of my messenger bag.

Yaya, who is wearing another white gown with blue trim, and a royal blue and white floral-patterned turban, kneels on a square velvet pillow in front of a small altar with candles lit. She signals for me to come near her and pats the mismatched pillow by her side, to indicate for me to kneel down as well.

"Dame la calabaza," she says, outstretching her arm. I gently pull out the gourd from my bag, take off the plastic wrap, and hand it to her.

She removes the lid, takes a whiff, and grins. "Sí, está maduro," she says.

She then takes a large wooden bowl from the altar and pours the contents of what was in my gourd into it. This bowl is much more ornate: there is a carving of a bird eating a fish on it. Titi Yaya places three palm nuts into it and swirls them around.

"This is called the Ifa Divination Vessel. I will use this to consult the orisha Orunmila, the god of wisdom. I want Orunmila to secure your blessings here."

What does one say to that?

"Thank you?" is all I can muster.

"You are my chosen one, Maya. I am not long for this earth. I am meant to teach you what I know, daughter of Yemaya, to continue the Santos legacy."

"But Titi, how can we make this happen? I can't just keep sneaking off to see you! I'm going to get into trouble!" I exclaim, heeding Kayla's advice.

"This is why I seek Orunmila's wisdom. He will show us the path," she says calmly. "Cierra los ojos y respira," she tells me, before closing her eyes and taking a deep breath. I copy her—mostly. OK, with one eye open.

She calls out, "Orunmila t'alade. Baba mo foti bale." Just like in my dreams, I do not recognize this language, but I assume it is ancient Yoruba.

She repeats the chant. A few minutes, and more deep breaths later, she repeats it again. Then, she opens her eyes and nods.

"Eso es. I asked Orunmila to show me the path to iré. Remember, in santería, we must always seek out balance and blessings. Right now, there is osogbo, unbalance and misfortune, between Chavela and me. He told me . . . I must make peace with my sister. Only then will the path be cleared," she finishes, before blowing out the candles.

"How are you going to do that?" I ask. "The last time I mentioned your name to her, she got real heated!" I'm remembering how Abuela took her anger out on that poor roasted chicken while yelling at me. She took the azabache that Titi Yaya had given me. She stormed out of the house. I can't bear to go through that again.

Titi rises from her floor pillow and I follow suit. The silver bangles on her wrist fall up and down her forearm with a soothing swoosh. "Ay, I know she still feels pain. I must show her that you will be safe under my care."

Abuela's words come back to me. "Titi, I just remembered something. Abuela said she doesn't need to lose another loved one to santería. What exactly does that mean? Did someone . . . die?"

Titi Yaya takes another deep breath and clasps her hands together in front of her chest. Her bracelets swoosh again. I brace myself to hear another "when you're older" lecture, but I am surprised by her response.

"There is an old dicho in santería: 'El hombre desaprueba lo que no puede realizar.' Human beings disapprove of things they cannot achieve."

From the altar, she picks up a small picture frame with an old photo showing a man and a woman. She points to the man. "Many years ago, your great-grandfather, my father, was a great babalawo . . . a very powerful healer. He teach me everything I know. I was his elegida.

Chavela did not understand santería, and was jealous that I got all my father's attention."

Then, she points to the woman in the picture. "One day, my mother became very sick. He treat her. Then he get sick. He wanted me to treat them with herbs and potions, just like our ancestors. So, I did. Your abuela was away dancing. She leave Dolores and your mamá with me. She would send money, but rarely visited. I raise those girls as if they were my own.

"I take care of everybody. Pero mis padres no want to go to hospital. They want to become spirits together. The orishas were calling them home. I hear it. I feel it. They died two hours apart, holding hands."

She puts the picture frame back on the altar, kisses her index and middle finger, then touches the photo with them.

"Chavela did not understand. From that point on, what I did was called "brujería." Your abuela took your Mami and Dolores back, and I never see them again . . . until last week when I see your Mami. I still miss them. Dolores could have been a great curandera. And I never meet Fausto and Trinidad . . . I see them for the first time when I come here."

Wow. I could see why Abuela would be upset. Suddenly, I feel so sad for her. Abuela lost both of her parents on the same day and she wasn't there. But mad enough to banish her own sister? I can't imagine losing Mami and Papi at the same time. I also can't imagine not being able to lean on Salma for support. I feel sad for Titi Yaya too—to lose her family all at once, including the nieces she raised. This was heavy.

"Is there anything I can do to help?"

I bite my lip, feeling helpless.

"No, nena. I will take care of this. Chacha es mi hermana. Just remember to always love your sister. You may be different. You may not agree. But you will always be sisters. And she is your only one. No vale la pena perderla."

I can see the pain now behind my great aunt's emerald eyes. It's not worth the heartbreak to lose a sister, regardless of the circumstance.

"Ahora, vete, muchacha," she says, shooing me away. "Basta for today. I must prepare myself."

I nod, hug Titi Yaya, then make my way downstairs.

Prepare herself for what?

Chapter 22

The Showdown

INSTEAD OF GOING HOME, I decide to go back to the café and join la ganga. My "cramps" have gone away, I announce before scooching my way into the booth next to Salma. Besides, I am suddenly hungry, and that mound of mofongo on the table is looking real good. Before I grab a forkful of mashed plantain and crispy pork crackling, I reach over and put my arm around my sister's shoulder, and give it a tight squeeze. Salma looks at me funny, but I don't care. No, scratch that. I do care. I care a lot. This is my family.

"What's gotten into you, ya weirdo?" Salma asks.

"¡Nada! I can't show my hermanita some love?" I ask back.

"Nah, you just wanna be closer to the mofongo."
Her accusation is only half true.

Just as we are finishing up our plates, a rush of hushed
silence fills the café. I look up, and the two remaining
customers are staring at the old woman in the head turban, who seems be floating by, wearing a flowing white and
blue gauze dress. Titi Yaya has come down from the apartment entrance and through the front of the café. Abuelo
follows her inside. I look over at my sister, my three cousins, and Trini, and they are looking at her like she is a
ghost. Tio Fausto and Titi Julia assuage the curious customers not to worry, though my aunt and uncle look a
little worried themselves that there might be a scene.

I gulp in anticipation of what might now be a
showdown—and it's all because of me. Mami and Abuela
enter the dining room from the kitchen, and Abuela stops
in her tracks when she sees her estranged sister standing
before her—in her own realm, on her turf. But before
Chacha can utter a word, Yaya holds her hand up.

"Chavela . . ." Yaya says softly. Not quite a plea—just
as a statement of fact.

Abuela's face softens at hearing her full name. Titi Yaya steps closer, until they are about two feet apart.

"It's been far too long. Necesitamos hacer la paz," Yaya states.

"Make peace? Why?" Abuela asks, her jaw tightening.

Titi Yaya says, "Mira, Chavela. I am a stranger. Estoy vieja. Estoy sola. I deserve family too."

"You can't just show up, after all these years, and make such demands! This is my family," Abuela retorts.

I get up from the booth and interrupt, suddenly emboldened. "Abuela, look around you. Look at the family you've created! There is so much love surrounding us every day . . . and yet we aren't allowed to know our own tía. She doesn't know us. But this is her family too."

"Maya, ya te dije: Stay out of grown-ups' business!" Abuela commands.

Titi Yaya responds, "No, Chavela, this is about Maya too. I need her. Maya . . . she can protect the family. But not without my help."

"Protect the family against what?" Abuela laughs.

"Change. Oya brings the winds of change. Upheaval. Turmoil. Loss. Tragedy. Maybe even death . . ." Yaya holds her sister's gaze.

I shudder at the worst-case scenario. Is it death that Oya was warning me about in my dream?

"Is that what happened the last time? You were not able to protect this family from loss then," Abuela says, hurt still palpable in her voice.

"There was nothing further I could do," Titi Yaya responds, her voice also cracking. "It was their time. And after that, I lost everyone I ever loved."

Abuela pauses, looking as though she's torn. I can see where Mami inherited that furrowed brow.

"I am worried for mi nieta. Solamente tiene trece años. She is just a child!" Abuela protests, walking over and putting a protective arm around me.

"She's old enough." Titi Yaya says. She shifts to one hip and asks, "How old were you when you knew you wanted to be a dancer?"

"Ay, that was a long time ago. No recuerdo eso." Abuela scoffs, her hands dismissing the thought.

"I do, hermana. You were four." Titi Yaya smiles wryly and holds up four fingers for emphasis.

"That's not the same thing!"

"No?"

Funny, now they sound like me and Salma arguing.

"What you want to teach her is not a vocation. Maya's going to go to college, get a degree, have a real career, make this family proud. Right, Maya?" Abuela asks, and then everyone else's eyes turn toward me.

"Well, yeah . . ." I didn't expect to have my life plan all figured out already. Can I at least get to high school first?

"Yes, but this will be a part of her. Learning santería will serve her well, just as it has served me," says Yaya. Then she adds, "Chavela, I am a healer. It is all that I know. Mine is an ancient practice that should not be lost. It is our family history. Es nuestra gente. Let me share our history with Maya. Teach her what I know. She can help the family survive for the next generation, after we are gone. She has aché. It is her destiny. Let her choose her own path."

Abuela now looks like she is running out of excuses. She turns to me, flustered, and asks, "Maya, is this what you want?"

I am flustered myself, but then the words find me. "I . . . yes. I want to follow my path, Abuela, and see where it takes me."

Just then, Mami, who's been silent the entire time, chimes in and puts her hands on my shoulders. "It's alright with me. And I'm Maya's mother. At the end of the day, Titi Yaya is family. Basta ya." She shares a look with Titi Yaya. It seems she has a soft spot for her long-lost aunt.

Everyone looks shocked as my Mami's words hang in the air, defying her own mother.

After a tense moment of silence, Abuela gives in. "Bueno, eso es. The decision has been made." She throws her hands up in makeshift defeat.

But this isn't enough for me. "Pero, Abuelita?" I say softly. "I also want you and Titi Yaya to make up. Is that possible?"

Abuela's back stiffens. "Ay, Maya. That is—how you say?—a tall order. Necesito tiempo."

Titi Yaya nods.

Bueno, at least it's a start.

And now, I can start my training!

I can't wait to call Papi and tell him. But for now, Tio Fausto points to the customers who are starting to trickle in for dinner. "We've gotta get the front and the back of the house ready."

"OK, hermano," Mami says, taking his cue. "Maya, Mamá, y Titi Yaya? Come with me to the kitchen."

"Can I come too?" Salma asks.

"Por supuesto, m'ija," Mami says.

As Mami, Abuela, and Salma start prepping the kitchen for dinner, Mami lays down the ground rules for which I am to be able to visit Titi Yaya.

"Numero uno, of course, is that your homework has to be done," Mami starts.

I sit on one of the metal stools against the wall. "And how often can I go?"

Yaya stands close to me. She smells wonderful. I drink her in.

"You can go today, but not every day. I don't want you to ignore the rest of your family. Plus, you have a big soccer match coming up. So, two, maybe three times a week at the most. Also, you can't be out late."

"OK. What about the weekends?" I ask.

"Oh, come on!" Salma protests.

"Salma, no te preocupes, I've got this. Maya, you're needed on the floor, just like everybody else. But maybe for an hour after the brunch rush dies down."

And that is how negotiations go down. Abuela remains silent in her protest as she chops green peppers. Salma, who is peeling garlic, seems to be a little on the jelly side. I know how she feels about me being "chosen" for anything. Meanwhile, she still has me doing her chores for another two weeks. So, who's the real winner here?

All the while, Titi Yaya smiles silently, relishing her first family moment—three generations of Santos women all together at once. Let the healing begin.

Chapter 23

Stories of the Gods

I FOLLOW THE PETITE VIEJITA up the stairs and back into her tiny studio apartment.

Turns out Titi Yaya is full of stories. Lots of them.

"So, is what you do actual magic?" I ask.

She fills a tea kettle with water from the sink and puts it on the burner.

"Well, the Yoruba believe in magic, but not in the way that you think of it. We believe that magic happens when we use our heads and our abilities to be so—¿cómo se dice?—brillante . . ." She pauses to emphasize that word. ". . . that we can frustrate evil. Magic transforms negativity to goodness. Hate to love. Weakness to strength," she explains.

"How does one actually become brilliant?" I ask. The tea kettle whistles.

She turns off the burner and pours two cups of boiling water, then adds an herb mixture. She hands me my cup.

"Mira, the Yoruba look at reality and divide it into two parts: forces that build up, and forces that tear down. We believe that once you are en conjunto with the positive forces—those that build up—you will have un destino más afortunado. My job as a curandera is simply to find balance for people."

"So, you deal in positive and negative forces. Got it," I say, before taking a sip.

"Sí, muy bien," Titi Yaya says with a soft chuckle. "Ven, siéntate," she commands, pointing me to one of her chairs.

She pulls a tattered book off the shelf. "The orishas will help you understand the way of the Ile Ife, where the Yoruba believe our civilization began, and where the orishas came to earth. Learning about the orishas can help you discover a different way of looking at how the world works," she tells me. "The Yoruba believe that without women and children, the world could not function."

"¿Que qué? You're not telling me I need to have a baby, are you?" I scrunch my nose as if I just smelled something bad.

"Claro que no," Titi Yaya laughs. "I do not have children, but I am still very blessed."

"OK, good," I say with relief. I don't know if a baby is in my future, so it's nice to know it's not a prerequisite.

She sits down next to me, and begins to tell me some patakís, which are the stories and legends of the Yoruba gods and goddesses. She opens the book and shows me pictures of some of the four hundred or so deities—some male, some female, some with no assigned gender at all. (So nonbinary people have been around for centuries—cool!)

Through these patakís, I learn of great warriors, great beauty, and lots of mischief. Yemaya is the mother to all orishas (except for her father, Oludumare, the Supreme Being, and Obatala, the father of fathers). And boy, tempers flare with these orishas! Somebody's always big mad at someone else for one thing or another. For example, Shango is the macho god of fire, thunderstorms, and war. At one point, Shango was two-timing, and married two of Yemaya's daughters back-to-back—he left Oya for Oba, the domestic goddess, and Oya, goddess of the four winds and the guardian of the cemetery, got very jealous and wanted to take revenge on the world. However, Yemaya forbade it, which created a rift between mother and daughter. (More dramatic than a telenovela!)

Since Oya became estranged from Yemaya, they have become rivals. Suddenly, I remember my dream about her, as well as Yaya telling Abuela Chacha that Oya would bring the winds of change, upheaval, and turmoil to our family. So, I perk up when Titi Yaya speaks about this fierce warrior, who never shows her face.

Of course, I love learning about Yemaya too, of whom I am a child. Mama Watta, she's sometimes called—the goddess of all Seven Seas from whom all rivers flow and rain drops. Mother to all. The saint she "hides behind" is the Virgin Mary. She is beautiful and serene, but fiercely protective of her many children, yet wary of love and marriage. (Kinda like me!)

Unfortunately, story time eventually has to end, because it's time for me to go already. We both get up from our chairs reluctantly.

"Is Yemaya Olukun still coming to you in your dreams?" Titi Yaya asks after I hug her and head for the door.

"Yes. But I also had a dream about Oya. It was more of a nightmare, really."

"¿Qué pasó?" she asks, with sudden concern on her face.

My voice is shaky as I audibly relive my dream. Titi Yaya nods silently along, rubbing up and down my arms to calm me down.

"Estará bien," she says.

"Is Oya evil?" I ask her as I stand in the doorway.

"No, m'ija. But she is to be respected," she tells me.

"What does Oya want from me? Why is she warning me about change?"

"Because change is inevitable. Pero ten cuidado, m'ija. Having this gift can sometimes be a burden, and you are still un iyabo. Worlds collide. Reality is not as sure as you think. Don't let the dream world ruin the real world. Oya is very powerful. Pero I will prepare you."

I look at the clock. "Carajo, I gotta go back to work," I say.

Titi Yaya gives me one last reassuring hug. Then I make my way downstairs and return to my non-magical world.

Chapter 24

The Initiation Begins

SUNDAY MORNING, I wake up early before anyone else (except Mami) and run to the café. I walk briskly through the kitchen, give Mami a quick kiss on the cheek, and head up the stairs. Titi Yaya is sitting at her kitchenette table nibbling on the pan dulce that she's having for breakfast. (Señora Infante has clearly just visited her.) She hands me one. Of course, I do not refuse.

Titi Yaya dusts the crumbs off her hands and announces, "Ahora, empezamos."

"Start what?" I ask as I take a hearty bite of sweetbread.

"Maya Beatriz, I am now tu iyatobi, your godmother. You are still an iyabo, an uninitiated. I will help you become an aborisha, as you learn the ways of the Yoruba tradition."

Wow, she's about to unlock all these ancient secrets! I can barely contain my excitement!

That is, until Titi Yaya hands me a broom.

"What do I do with this?" I ask her.

Titi looks at me like I have three heads.

"Pues, barre, m'ija. Eswep!" She claps three times for emphasis.

Grrrrreat, first Salma's chores. Now this?!? I stay losing.

I finish my pan dulce and reluctantly take the broom from her hand. After I sweep her floors, Titi Yaya has me wash dishes. Some initiation this is! Then, she teaches me how to crack coconuts open. At least I can work out my frustrations with a hammer.

Before I know it, it is time for me to go. The brunch rush will be starting soon, and the coffee station awaits.

"Hasta la próxima, nena," Yaya says.

Gee, maybe I'll be doing laundry the next time, I think to myself.

As if reading my mind, she says next, "Ten paciencia. Cada tarea tiene valor."

OK, maybe my newfound godmother isn't a tiny tyrant after all.

FROM THAT POINT ON, every time I am allowed to go up and see her, Yaya gives me some mundane household chore to do. This is part of my initiation, she tells me. I suppose I'm doing a good deed by helping an old woman tidy up, and she does look tired sometimes, I think to myself, but she explains this is part of my role as an iyabo.

In between tasks, she always tells me or teaches me something. One day, she shows me the best way to cut an eggplant as she tells me another pataki about the orisha Oshun, the goddess of love and beauty, who radiates in amber and is known for her intelligence and charm. She reminds me of Trini a little bit. Maybe Oshun is her orisha?

Another day, Titi Yaya teaches me how to debone a chicken, while telling me about the Ibeyi—the twin gods, the children of Shango—who can either bring happiness when they are happy, or misery if they are dissatisfied.

Titi Yaya doesn't seem to like when I ask too many questions, but rather wants to let the knowledge wash over me and seep in me. I still don't quite understand what it all means, but frankly, I like just hanging out with her. She is serious and mysterious, with an enchanting aura about her. When she laughs, it is like a song, and I can't help but join in. She seems to be relishing the time lost with all her family in hanging out with me, her grand-niece and newfound goddaughter. There is something magical about her, even though she doesn't actually perform magic—at least the kind that kids typically think of. I remember her definition of magic: to be so dazzling so as to frustrate evil. I kind of love that. But how do I do that exactly?

"When am I going to get to do some magic or something?" I blurt out one day, bursting into her clean-because-of-me apartment.

"Ohhhh, you want to do some magic, eh?" She laughs. "Bueno, ven acá."

I kneel next to her at the altar, and she places a handful of cowrie shells into an empty coconut shell. She hands it to me.

"What do I do with this?" I ask.

"Clear your mind. Take a deep breath," she instructs. She breathes deeply as an example. "Shake it, then throw the shells on the floor."

"Oh, like dice?"

"Eso, sí." A smile creeps across her face as she learns a new word in English. "Like dice."

After I toss the cowrie shells on the floor, she studies the pattern and measures the distance between them with her finger.

"This is called divination," Titi Yaya explains.

"Ohhhh . . . Does that mean that you can see the future?" I ask.

"I see the energy and the path that Eleggua shows me. Eleggua is the messenger orisha who stands at the crossroads of fate. He can only speak the truth. This reading will reveal whether you are in a state of iré—balance and blessings—or osogbo, unbalance and misfortunes. The nature and origin of that iré or osogbo will also be revealed."

Her brow furrows like a true Santos. "I see osogbo ahead," she says.

"Did you ask Eleggua a specific question?" I ask tentatively.

"I asked about you. There is some imbalance or misfortune in your path," she whispers as she reaches for my chin and studies me closer.

I rack my brain, trying to think of all that is going on in my life. Things at school seem fine. Salma and I have a truce for the time being. Kayla and I are just starting something. Sure, Abuela still seems annoyed at the whole estranged sister situation, but I'm able to visit Titi Yaya now without verbal protest. The only thing I can think of is my upcoming soccer tournament. The azabache spared me last game, but then Abuela confiscated it.

I tell Titi Yaya about Gina Sardino, and how she seemed to always have it in for me.

"This Gina, she wants to hurt you." She isn't asking a question.

"I guess," I answer. Sure, Gina is mad jealous of me, and a bully. So—by definition—she is my nemesis. But I am not about to miss out on the big game because the opposing goalie wants to fade me. Then again, the last time I faced her, I wound up in the hospital.

"Chavela still has your azabache, verdad?" Titi says. Again, she already knows the answer.

"Yes, she took it. So, what do I do to protect me?" I ask.

"We ask the orishas to give you good fortune. Oya brings change, but Yemaya . . . she will always protect her daughter. Ven. Vamos a ver."

I take the three steps it takes to get to her kitchenette. She has all kinds of spices and ingredients that smell so good—fresh oregano, fennel, basil, and thyme, just to name a few. Just as I start inhaling their rich aromas, she lights a cigar. My nose scrunches up at the smell of the smoke. Then she hands me a butternut squash and a knife.

"Cut the calabaza in half and hollow it out. I will make an ofrenda para buena fortuna."

"A good luck spell? Now we're talking," I say while rubbing my hands together in anticipation.

While I clean out the squash, Titi Yaya takes out honey, sugar, cloves, cinnamon sticks, and a bottle of rum. She takes the cigar out of her mouth long enough to pull un trago of rum, then pours some out into a glass bowl.

She mixes in all the other ingredients and pours them into the now hollowed-out calabaza.

"Oh god, am I going to have to eat this concoction?" I ask, again scrunching up my nose again in potential disgust.

"No, you don't eat it, m'ija," she says, chuckling. "I will take it to the river tomorrow morning and make la ofrenda before your game."

"Good, because if I have rum on my breath when I get home, Mami would kill me!" I reply with a nervous laugh. "So, what do I do to make this magic happen?"

Yaya lets out a sing-songy chuckle and goes to her altar to retrieve a small vial. "You think you can put this on Gina?"

"Hmmm, lemme think. Maybe when we line up for the coin toss. Does it have to go anywhere specific? I don't want to get too close. She might bite me."

"¡Dios mío! ¡Qué bárbaro!" she exclaims. "M'ija, just get some on her body. Quizás el brazo."

"Her arm. Got it." I hide the vial inside my sports bra. Then, after a pause, I ask, "Uh, you gonna tell me what this is or what it does?"

She chuckles melodically again. "Mala fortuna. You get good luck, she gets bad luck."

"Ohhhh . . . OK. Cool. Anything else?"

"Tomorrow morning, take nine pennies outside, face in the direction of the river, then throw the pennies over your shoulder. Don't look back."

"OK, got it," I say. I suddenly realize that from this point on, there is no going back to life as I knew it before.

Chapter 25
Buena y Mala Fortuna

I WAKE UP Saturday morning feeling uneasy. Normally, I don't get nervous before a game, but there's more than just my return and the championship on the line—it's my health and well-being too! Coming off a concussion, I suddenly feel a little naked and exposed without my azabache. I haven't had the courage to ask Abuela for it back yet.

After breakfast at the café, I excuse myself and ask if I could go upstairs. "Yes, but don't be long," Mami says. I take my plate into the kitchen, place it in the rack next to the dishwasher, and then take the back stairs two at a time. I gently knock on the door, but it's already half open—I just have to push it a few inches to enter.

"Bueno, I just returned from the river. I gave Yemaya your ofrenda," Titi Yaya says with her back to me. I guess she senses my presence.

Titi Yaya turns around with a hot cup of tea in her hands, which she hands over.

"Toma. For strength," she says. Oddly, she looks like she could use some extra strength too. She seems tired.

I take a sip. "Ugh! This tastes awful!"

"Not everything can be delicioso. Toma," she urges. I manage to not throw up taking a few more swigs.

"OK, Titi. I gotta go. My game starts soon."

"Pues, m'ija, buena suerte. Don't forget los centavos!"

"Got 'em!" I say, jingling my pocket for emphasis.

I HUSTLE DOWNSTAIRS, kiss Mami on the cheek, and dart into the main dining room to grab Ini and Mini to come be my cheering section again.

"Take Erasmo with you!" Titi Julia reminds us.

"Come on, Momo," I say.

"Yay!" He jumps up from the booth and darts outside ahead of us.

On the way to the soccer field, everything seems brighter. The sky looks bluer. The grass looks greener. The air smells fresher, which is saying something in New York City, where summers usually stink of hot asphalt and garbage. I feel alert and alive. Just when I enter the park, I remember to take out the pennies from my pocket. I stop walking, face east, toss the pennies over my shoulder, and remember not to look back. I must continue walking toward my destiny.

"Heeey, what was that for?" Ini asks.

"For good luck," I say with a smile.

"For you? Or for whoever finds that money?" asks Mini.

"Both, I guess!" And I truly am guessing at this point.

"It's not like anyone will get rich finding a few pennies," says Ini.

"I'll take the money!" Mo turns around to run toward the coins on the ground.

"No! Leave them alone!" I warn him. Somehow, I don't think that's how this spell works, and I don't want to jinx it.

Mo pouts as we walk the rest of the way to the field. Then Ini, Mini, and Mo take a seat on the sidelines.

Coach greets me as I walk to our side of the field. "Good to see you, champ. How you feelin'?"

"I feel pretty OK," I answer. "Not looking forward to facing Gina again though."

"Don't let her get into your head. That's what bullies want," Coach says.

"Besides, I got your back," says Kayla as she comes up behind me and puts her hands on my shoulders. I look back at her face and smile.

"Listen, Maya, you gotta do everything in your power today to protect yourself against injury. You cannot afford to have three concussions in four short months. Forget the game—this is your life we're talking about," Coach says sternly.

"Yeah, maybe ease up on going Air Maya today?" Kayla pleads.

Coach and Kayla are right. I'm not about to give in . . . yet I need to be cautious. That's how I'll find the balance Titi Yaya talks about. I pat the vial hidden inside my sports bra for good measure. I don't know exactly what's about to go down, but I feel like the orishas are on my side.

During the lineup, I make sure to stand directly opposite Gina. I cup the vial in my hand and disguise it in between my towel and water bottle. After the coin toss (tails), I pretend to trip. I aim my hands so that both the water and the vial contents will land on Gina's arm.

"You stupid klutz!" she shouts as she wipes herself off. I don't say sorry as I jog to the sidelines and join my team's huddle.

As is expected during a championship match, it's a tight game. At the end of the first half, it is still zero–zero. Despite Ini and Mini's cheers, Gina thwarts every attempt I make at goal and taunts me after each save—of course, always just out of earshot of the refs. I keep telling myself not to get flustered; she is just trying to get into my head. I keep wondering when that bad luck potion Titi Yaya gave me will start to take effect. Seven minutes into the second half, my wish is granted.

Kayla dribbles the ball down the left side of the field. I am running down the center, angling to open myself for the pass. I see an opening at the top of the penalty box. I make a hard right and signal to Kayla to pass it to me. She kicks the ball about four feet ahead of me, and I sprint to trap it. That's when Gina exits the goalie box and comes rushing toward me.

"Focus, Maya," I mutter to myself.

I can tell Gina is gearing up to slide tackle me. For a brief second, I steel myself for impact. But at the last minute, something (or someone) tells me to jump. I jackknife myself into the air headfirst and hear the crowd gasp—*oh noooo*! I can't afford to have another head injury! But before I can panic, I tuck my head, stretch out my hands and arms, and tumble into a graceful somersault, gaining enough energy to propel myself back up on my feet. Wow! I've never done that before! Then, the ball magically slows down and rolls right in front of me. I cut inside, aim, and take an easy shot at the empty goal. Score! The crowd erupts into cheers. The twins do a little dance. Mo joins them for a family jig.

"Gina! Keep your head in the game!" the Honey Badgers' coach shouts as Gina stands back up and dusts herself off. Clearly, the woman is growing tired of Gina going after me, instead of the ball. That tells me I need to find my way to the red zone as much as possible.

Another seven minutes later, Kayla and I are making another break for it, passing the ball back and forth all the way up field. Again, once I cross the penalty box, it's like Gina acts like a dog smelling red meat. She comes out to tackle me again, leaving the goal wide open. Kayla easily scores from the left side of the penalty box with her right foot.

"Great job, Kayla! Way to follow through!" Coach yells.

"Sardino, get over here. Now!" Gina's coach barks. "You're benched. Ashley, you're up!"

"Mala fortuna," I say aloud to myself.

Gina sulks her way over to the sidelines, where the backup goalie is warming up. Ashley isn't nearly as good or as menacing, so I am relieved my imminent threat was benched. In the last few minutes of the game, my teammates and I score two more goals easily, just to add to Gina's humiliation. The championship is ours! Still, putting a bully in her place—and saving my hide in the process—feels even sweeter.

I can't wait to tell Titi Yaya the news. Or does she know the result already?

Chapter 26

Something's Not Right

AFTER THE TEAM relishes our victory, it's time for la familia to continue the celebration at the café. And perfect timing—we arrive an hour before the dinner shift begins. Slaying dragons on the soccer pitch usually works up quite an appetite, so I am more than ready for a table full of cuchifritos like alcapurrias (fried mini beef fritters), rice, beans, plátanos maduros, and roasted pernil that Abuela prepared the night before. Pork always puts everyone in a good mood.

Trini sits down with us kids, just like old times. Not even Salma seems to mind the extra attention paid to me. She's laughing along and taking in the yumminess of all the food. In between bites, the twins regale the fam with the highlights of the game. Of course, my goal is the most talked about.

"You looked like Megan Rapinoe out there," says Ini.

"With a touch of Simone Biles." Mini adds.

"Swwwwiiiissssssshhhhh!" Mo chimes in. He just loves to sound out the word.

"Where'd you learn how to flip like that, Maya?" Salma asks. "You never took gymnastics."

I shrug my shoulders. "I dunno," I say. "It just felt like the right thing to do."

"What was up with Gina? Why did she get benched?" Trini asks.

"I think her coach got mad that she was so hellbent on going after me instead of the ball. It cost them the game. Too bad, so sad for them. Lucky me."

Luck! What Yaya said! I have to see her!

I ask Mami if I can be excused to go upstairs, and she quietly says yes. In fact, she tells me to bring her a plate. I feel Abuela's eyes following me as I fix the plate and take it upstairs on my way to the apartment. I thought the door would be ajar like it normally is when I visit, but this time it's closed. I knock. No answer. I knock louder. Still no answer.

"Titi Yaya?"

No answer again. I balance the plate in one hand and turn the doorknob. Luckily, it is unlocked. I glance around the room. She's not in the kitchen. She's not at her at her altar. She's not sitting in one of her chairs. But in the twin bed tucked in the corner of the room, with a sheer curtain closing it off from the rest of the studio apartment, I see her silhouette lying down. I set the plate down on the kitchen table and walk over to the bed.

"Titi?" I whisper as I inch closer. Something's not right. I kneel in front of her and gently shake her shoulder. Her eyes flutter open, and she smiles at me weakly.

"Hola, nena," she whispers.

"Are you OK?" I ask.

"Ay, soy vieja. Sometimes I tire. Muy cansada." Her voice is faint.

Now I have the Santos Furrowed Brow. I knew she looked tired earlier! But is there something else going on?

"¿Ganaste?" she asks with a knowing, albeit weak smile.

"Yes, we won. And your good luck/bad luck potions worked, I guess."

Her eyelids are getting droopy again. "Bueno. I show you how to make soon."

I'm still worried, but I feel uncomfortable disturbing her sleep. "Maybe I should go."

Titi Yaya inhales deeply, then exhales. "Lo siento, hoy descanso. Today, I rest."

"OK, I'll leave the food in the fridge. I'll check on you mañana." I reach over and kiss her forehead.

"Gracias, m'ija."

I get up, grab the plate, cover it with plastic wrap, and put in the fridge. As I make my way out, I suddenly think about Oya and the winds of change. Could Titi be involved in this? Tragedy, loss, death . . . could it be? Might Titi Yaya be getting sick?

I leave the apartment with one urgent thought: I have to talk to Abuela. She needs to make amends with her sister—before it's too late. It's up to me to make it happen. And time might be running out.

Chapter 27

Ayuda

WHEN I COME DOWNSTAIRS, Abuela is in the café's kitchen cleaning up. I take a deep breath—it's now or never.

"Can I help?" I ask.

She looks at me quizzically. "You're the champion today, m'ija. You don't have to help me today. Now, tomorrow will be a different story," she teases.

"No, I want to help," I say as I grab a pot to dry.

"What's gotten into you, Maya?" I have a feeling Abuela can see right through me.

I don't know how to start, so I just blurt it out: "Have you decided whether you are going to make peace with Yaya or not?"

Abuela's back stiffens and she stops wiping down the counter to turn around and face me. "Maya, I don't see how this is any of your business."

"Lo siento, Abuela, pero I have this feeling." I reach up and place the pot on the hanging rack.

"¿Qué qué? What feeling?" Her hands are on her hips now.

I gulp. I am scared to say it out loud, because maybe if I voice it, it will suddenly come true. But I feel it in my soul.

"I think Titi Yaya is sick. Maybe she might be dying even."

"A healer who can't heal herself?" she scoffs. Then she softens. "Espera . . . ¿Moribunda? What makes you say that? Did she tell you something?"

"No, I told you. It's just a feeling. When I went upstairs just now, she seemed very weak."

"Well, es una vieja like me. We old people tire easily."

"Pero this seems different . . . She couldn't get out of bed."

Abuela raises her eyebrows in sudden concern. But then, she starts to cough herself. It starts out slow, but turns into such a fit she has to sit down on one of the stools in the kitchen.

"Are you OK, Abuela?" I feel my brow furrowing for the second time in less than fifteen minutes over someone I love. Two sick Santos sisters . . . ?

"Ay, I've had this cough that just won't go away," she says, after it dies down.

"Maybe you should get that checked out, Abuela," I say, sounding a bit like Mami.

"Ay, no." She waves me off, dismissing the thought of it being anything serious.

"Anyway, I just wanted you to know about Titi Yaya, just in case." I want my Abuela to take me seriously, but I know she won't.

"OK, you told me. You can go now." She tries to shoo me away again.

I can tell Abuela is trying to shut me down, but I dig my heels in. "Abuela, Titi Yaya is good. She has been good to me. She deserves the benefit of the doubt. She deserves forgiveness. She's your sister!"

"That is not for you to decide, Maya. What do you know? You are still a child," she says, now totally dismissing me.

"Well, I know *this*. It's that the past few weeks with Titi Yaya have been, well, wonderful. I love having her as part of my family. *Our* family. It would be nice if you did too," I say, adding ominously, "before it's too late."

Maybe a little guilt trip is the ticket?

Abuela sighs. "Maya, if you only knew . . ."

"I already know, Abuelita," I say softly, so as not to make her upset again. It doesn't work.

"Oh. You two have gotten close, I see." She stands up, riling back up, which makes her cough again. After this coughing fit stops, she asks sarcastically, "Anything else you want to tell me?"

"Only that I know what it's like to have a sister. Salma and I may not always get along, but I'm always going to love her and have her back. I can't imagine it any other way."

Abuela sits back down to regain her strength. "Maya, you are still young, and very naive. Adulthood changes things sometimes."

"But why does it have to? You're always telling us about the importance of family. Why does it not apply to you?"

Abuela's eyes narrow at first, as if to yell at me for my insolence, but then she starts coughing again.

"Abuela, why don't you go home and lay down? I can clean up, really."

She starts to protest, but instead gets hit with another wave of coughing, so she gives in. "Alright, m'ija. If you say so."

She stands up, removes her apron, grabs her purse, and heads home.

Oh, man, this is really bad. First, Titi Yaya becomes ill. Now Abuela isn't well? Could the two somehow be related? Everything is happening so fast, and the fact that they're sick at the same time seems like more than just a coincidence. After all, their parents died within hours of each other. Could it happen again? I suddenly feel burdened being the only one in my immediate family with this knowledge. But who else can I turn to?

BACK AT HOME the next morning, Abuela emerges from downstairs. She looks worse—weaker and paler. Her breathing is labored, almost wheezing. It seems weird that with everything that happened with her parents, and having survived a pandemic, Abuela is still so distrusting of doctors. It might just be a generational thing, but I know she won't get checked out, so I don't bother to ask. I go to give her a hug. She is warm, like she is running a fever.

"Abuela, are you OK?" I ask.

"Eh, no sé." I am shocked by her response. She is usually too proud of a woman to ever admit defeat to an illness. This is the closest she would admit to feeling like poop.

"Abuelita, go lie back down. I can whip up breakfast for Salma and me. No te preocupes."

Again, she doesn't put up a fight. She just turns around and heads back to her bedroom downstairs.

I grab the box of cereal and pour it into two bowls. I add milk to mine, grab a spoon, and start munching while I walk to the kitchen table. Salma will complain about having a cold breakfast, and frankly, I don't care. I am more concerned about my grandmother and my great aunt.

As if on cue, Salma comes downstairs, sees the cereal box and bowl, and frowns.

"Oh man, cereal? I thought Abuela would at least make us some oatmeal."

I walk back to the kitchen counter to pour myself a second bowl to sop up the rest of the milk. "She isn't feeling well, so cold cereal it is. Deal with it, Sal."

"What's wrong with Abuela?" Salma asks, suddenly concerned.

"Dunno. I'm worried, though," I say, plopping back down at the kitchen table. I am racking my brain wondering how I can help, but nothing comes to mind.

"Oh no! What can we can do?" Salma asks.

"Dunno. You know how Abuela is. At least she agreed to rest."

"Yeah, you're right," Salma says.

I was hoping I had enough time to head over to see Titi Yaya before school, but Mami is already bugging us to hurry up. It will have to wait until the afternoon after school.

ONCE OUT THE DOOR, I drag behind the rest of la ganga. And then it hits me: I need to talk to Señora Infante alone. When we arrive at the bakery, I let everyone get their rolls first. "Y'all go on ahead of me. I'll catch up."

I predict the side eye that comes from Salma. "OK, just don't be late. You know how Mami feels about tardies," she warns.

"Yeah, I know, Sal. Good looking out. I got it though," I assure her.

I wait until I hear the sleigh bell ring on the door as my sister and cousins head out.

Señora Infante hands me my leche con café. "What's on your mind, Maya?"

I don't know how to broach the subject, so I just let the words roll out in a frenzied mess. "Both Abuela and Titi are suddenly really sick and I'm worried they're both dying at the same time just like their parents did and Oya told me not to be afraid of the winds of change but I *am* afraid but I am still an iyabo so I don't know enough to know what to do!"

"Ohhhh, wow. That *is* a lot, nena!" she says, taking a sip of her own coffee. "Pues, this sounds like it could be osogbo. Do you know what that is?"

I think for a few seconds. "Yes, Titi Yaya taught me. It means there's an imbalance."

"Exactamente. They both need to heal from their wounds at the same time, to bring iré again. Is there any way you can get them together in the same room? That might help things settle quicker.

"I don't know. I think so. Maybe after school."

"OK, well, you try. And I'll pray."

I wrap my arms around her soft middle. "Thank you, Señora." And I dart off to school to beat the late bell.

At lunch, my mind is preoccupied. Kayla asks what's wrong, and I don't know what to tell her, so I just say, "My Abuela and my titi are both sick." It's true, but there is a weightiness to it that I just can't explain just yet.

"I'm so sorry, Maya. I hope they both get better soon," Kayla says, rubbing my back. Even if it's temporary, I feel a little better.

When I return home from school, Abuela is still in bed with a full-blown fever. Mami is trying to convince her to go to the hospital.

"Don't be so stubborn, Mamá," Mami says. "Am I going to have to call an ambulance?"

Abuela shakes her head vehemently.

"People your age die every day of the flu and pneumonia, Mamá! Or worse—la corona!" Mami turns to me and says in exasperation, "I don't know what to do."

I do. I only need permission to do so.

I go to the other side of Abuela's bed. I stroke the errant hairs that are matted to my grandmother's forehead. I lean in and whisper my plea, "Can I get Titi Yaya?"

Mami sighs. "Ay, nena . . ."

Abuela puts up a hand in protest. She then turns her head to look me in the eye, and slowly nods.

Chapter 28

Las Hermanas Santos

I RUN AS FAST as my size-eleven feet can take me to Café Taza. I bypass any familial greetings in the dining room and bound up the kitchen stairs two at a time. Titi Yaya has already opened the door before I can even knock on it. She still looks under the weather, but the look on her face shows a sense of urgency.

"Chavela. Está enferma." She says it as a statement of fact instead of a question, but I answer anyway.

"Yes."

"Pues, vámonos." She picks up a satchel that sits ready by the door.

I take the satchel from her hand and help her down the stairs. Then she follows me down the block. Though she moves slower than usual, she walks with purpose down Fulton Street until we get to our brownstone.

Mami is there to greet us. With the satchel still in my hand, I guide Titi Yaya downstairs to Abuela's room.

"Hermana," says Abuela, and holds out her hand.

"Hermana," Titi Yaya repeats. She takes Abuela's outstretched hand with her right, and feels her forehead with her left. She then puts her hand atop Abuela's chest, which rises and falls for several labored breaths.

"Dame la bolsa," Titi Yaya instructs me. I do as I am told. I am truly apprenticing for Yaya now, but now, the stakes are high, as it's over my own Abuela's sickbed. I have wanted to be in this position and waited for this moment, but not like this.

"Now, it is time to cure illness—this is called asojano," Yaya explains.

She opens the bag and pulls out several large banana leaves. "Unfold these," she instructs. I take them to the foot of the bed and lay them flat.

She then takes out a small mortar and pestle. "Ven. Hold this," she tells me. They are heavier than I thought. She pours an herb concoction out of a glass jar into the mortar.

"Dame la mano del mortero." I hand her the pestle and then use both hands to hold the mortar. She muddles the mysterious herb while I act as a human shelf. I am witnessing salsa magic in real time.

Yaya unbuttons Abuela's house dress and massages the concoction onto her bare chest.

"What's this? Some kind of ancient Vicks or something?" Latines will use Vicks Vaporub for anything that ails you.

Titi Yaya smiles and says softly, "Quizás."

But a few minutes later, Abuela's cough seems to subside.

"Dame las hojas," she says and points across the bed. I hand her the banana leaves. She then wraps them around Abuelita's torso, making her look like a modified mummy. Then she puts the covers over the banana leaves and tucks the blankets around her.

"Now what?" I ask.

"Ahora, esperamos." Now, we wait. And/or hope. Esperar means both in Spanish. I've always found that oddly beautiful.

~ ~ ~

THAT ASOJANO RITUAL seems to have helped Titi Yaya regain some of her strength. So, we go upstairs to the kitchen, where Mami is making tea.

"¿Quieres té?" Mami asks her aunt.

Titi Yaya nods and smiles.

Mami pours three mugs of hot water over chamomile tea bags. I watch the steam rise and kiss Titi Yaya's face like she is emerging from a cloud. This is how she looks whenever she appeared in my dreams—soft and serene, like the ocean at low tide. If Trini were here, she would totally draw her.

Titi Yaya breaks the silence by asking my mom a question out of the blue: "¿Todavía bailas?"

Mami looks incredulous for a moment, before a single tear falls down her cheek. "You . . . remember?"

"Claro que sí. Eras como tu mamá."

"Wait a minute," I say. "Mami, how come you never told us you were a dancer?"

"Ay nena, I was young." More tears fall.

"Una bailarina bella," Titi Yaya says, with a hint of pride in her voice.

"Like, actual ballet?" I ask. Now that I think about it, Mami has killer legs just like Abuela. She just doesn't show them off very much.

"Yeah," she says, wiping her eyes. "I used to have dreams of performing at Lincoln Center. That was a long time ago. Then I met your father, had you girls. Your uncle needed help with the restaurant, so I hung up my ballet slippers and traded them in for an apron to help the family business."

She shrugs nonchalantly and takes a sip of tea. "Now, don't get me wrong: I love my life and I love you girls more than anything in this world. Everything changes."

Huh. I never knew that about Mami. She sacrificed her passion for the sake of the family. What other family secrets are there, I wonder?

For the moment, we sip our tea in silence. And wait for a miracle to happen. Esperamos.

Chapter 29

Homecoming

IT TAKES TWO DAYS to witness the healing process. By that time, Papi and Titi Dolores have decided to fly in from California to be with us in Brooklyn, because they too are worried about Abuela. Salma and I both know they are here for a somber occasion, so we have to temper our glee. But it will be so, so good to see them.

Salma and I come straight home after school in anticipation of their arrival just moments before. We bust through the door and practically trip over each other to see who can jump into Papi's arms first. (It's me.) Papi is tall and slender with thick, wavy hair, and looks very professorial in his glasses. It has been four months since we last saw him and he's gotten a nice tan.

Titi Dolores has a casual Southern California vibe, her brown hair streaked with gold and her skin kissed by the sun. She looks happy to see us, and gives Salma and me big hugs in the hallway. But I notice she has the same Santos Furrowed Brow as she worries about her mom being seriously sick.

"How's Chacha?" Papi asks.

"She seems a little better, but still has a fever," Mami says.

"Should we take her to the hospital?" asks Titi Dolores.

Mami hesitates, then says, "Creo que sí. We can't have history repeating itself."

"Pues, vamos. Let's go get her," says Papi. "I'll carry her if I have to."

But when we all go downstairs, Abuela is sitting in the middle of the couch in her living room slurping sopa. Her fever has broken and her face has color in it again.

"Dolores! Eduardo! ¡Qué sorpresa!" Abuela says boisterously. "Did someone tell you I was dying or something?" she asks in a lilting tone.

"No, Chacha, I just wanted to see how my favorite girl was doing!" I swear, Papi could charm a pig to his own slaughter.

"You know how I am, Ma, always worrying," says Dolores.

"Estoy bien, gracias a mi hermana. Eduardo, have you met Yaya?"

"No, only heard the legends, like everybody else," Papi says.

Abuela ignores that slightly shady remark and calls her sister over. "Yaya! ¡Ven aquí!"

Yaya, who just two days ago herself looked tired and listless, enters the living room just as perky as her older sister. Suddenly, both Santos sisters look vibrant and healthy, as if their well-being is somehow symbiotic. And—given the family history, and the beautiful mysticism of santería—it probably is. I can't help but smile at this magical moment.

"Ay, sí. El marido de Soledad. Encantada," Yaya says and extends her hand before Papi can even be introduced.

"Mucho gusto, señora," Papi croons and kisses the back of her hand.

Titi Yaya, with her eyes welling up, turns to my aunt. "Y mi querida Dolores, ¿cómo estás?" Titi Yaya hasn't seen her beloved niece in more than two decades.

"Mejor ahora, tía," she says with a relieved smile. Titi Yaya walks over to her and lovingly pats her cheek.

Now that the situation is no longer an emergency, Titi Dolores can tell everyone about what my cousins Taina and Tommy are up to in California. Taina is playing tennis while Tommy is all about basketball. Both are begging for a dog.

"I'm jealous Papi is out there with you," I say.

"Well, we don't see him much. He's working very hard to protect the immigrants at the border who are seeking asylum," Titi Dolores says.

Papi sighs weightily and runs a hand through his thick waves. "It's absolutely horrific what's happening at the border," he says. "It's not just Mexicans; it's people traveling treacherous routes from Central America and Haiti, who are running away from oppressive regimes and gang violence. They need to be treated like decent human beings, and I am doing everything I can to see that they are," he adds. "But I'll be home before you know it, mis hijas."

"Papi, did I tell you I started playing the guitar?" Salma asks excitedly.

"You sure did!" Papi returns her enthusiasm. "Your mom says you're pretty good, too! Why don't you get it and play something for me?"

"OK!" She bustles upstairs. I haven't seen Salma hustle so fast before. Then again, I haven't ever seen Salma so hyped about something before.

I am smiling at this impromptu family reunion. Dolores is hugging Titi Yaya, her long-lost aunt. Mami hugs Dolores, her sister who moved across the country. Dolores sits next to Abuela and hugs her mom. And then the two matriarchs of the family, Abuela and Yaya, hold hands. In this moment, each Santos woman, it seems, has been given a reprieve . . . another chance at reconciling in this lifetime, to rededicate themselves to being a family again. And to think, I helped make this moment possible. Maybe this is my aché, and my purpose—to be the bridge between the generations, the glue that holds the family together, and the keeper of traditions.

Just then, the rest of the family—Abuelo, Tio Fausto, Titi Julia, Trini, Ini, Mini, and Mo—come downstairs and crowd into Abuela's living room.

"Abuela!" Mo shouts. He tries to climb in her lap, but Tio Fausto grabs him and thwarts his effort.

Abuela pats him on the head and gives his cachetes a pinch. "Hola, querido Erasmo."

"I closed the café for a few hours to come see how you were doing, mamá," Tio Fausto says.

I know this is a big deal for my uncle. He's giving up money. But this is his mother. Family before business. Siempre. Always. Siempre.

"Mi amor," Abuelo says. He rushes to the couch and sits down next to Abuela. He reaches for her hand, then kisses it tenderly.

Abuela clears her throat to get everybody's attention. "Oye, I want to say something," she says to the group, before turning to her sister. "Hermana, discúlpame. I have deeply wronged you. I have judged you and banished you from our family. I was wrong. So wrong. I misplaced my own guilt and grief and put it all on you. I vow to work on making things better between us until the day I die. Te prometo."

Titi Yaya beams. "Mi hermana. The only thing that matters is that I have my sister again. That I have my family again." There are tears in both Santos sisters' eyes.

Mo looks at Titi Yaya, as if he's trying to solve a puzzle in his head. Then he blurts out, "Are you the witch?"

"Erasmo!" Titi Julia, looking mortified, grabs him and shushes him. "Discúlpele, señora."

"Está bien," Titi Yaya says with a grin. She looks at Mo and says gently, "M'ijito, I am a healer. I heal your Abuela."

"Oh, cool! That means I love you!" Mo gives Titi Yaya a big bear hug. Everybody has a good laugh. Leave it to Mo the Innocent Imp to break the ice into tiny pieces.

Then, Ini, Mini, and Trini introduce themselves formally to their aunt. Titi Yaya gives each one a hug.

Salma comes downstairs with her guitar. She sits in Abuelo's recliner, balances the guitar on her lap, checks her fingers on the guitar's neck to make sure they're on the right strings, and starts to strum a Spanish tune. Eight counts in, and I think, *Hey, she is pretty good!*

Papi has his arm draped around Mami's shoulder and they are both smiling proudly. Tio Fausto and Titi Julia also are holding each other close. Abuelo, Abuela, and

Titi Dolores are still sitting on the couch and tapping their toes to the rhythm. I think if Abuela was feeling one hundred percent, she and Abuelo would be dancing. Instead, Ini and Mini break out into one of their routines. Trini picks up Mo and twirls him around. Titi Yaya is smiling broadly—soaking it all in.

And I, of course, am overjoyed. In the Santos-Calderon-Montenegro household, there is finally iré. Balance.

I watch my hermanita concentrating on hitting all the right chords on her guitar. It sounds like she is finally finding her thing. Salma and I are so different, but that doesn't mean we don't have anything in common. Maybe she has a better understanding of my connection to Titi Yaya and santería now. Maybe I shouldn't judge her too harshly either, and give her the benefit of the doubt. Sure, siblings are always going to squabble, but there's no need for beef. As sisters, we can have our differences, but there should never be a rift that is too deep to overcome.

After the song and a round of applause, Abuela turns to me. "Maya, I believe I have something that belongs to you," she says.

She reaches into the drawer of the end table and pulls out the azabache.

"You have showed great courage and determination. I cannot keep you from your destiny. Yaya will show you the way." And with that, Abuela hands me the stone.

Wow. My abuela is giving me her blessing to continue my apprenticeship with Titi Yaya.

Maybe there's more to this magic thing than just cowrie shells, an ancient language, and special herbal potions. Aché is in the way you carry yourself, and the way you treat others. If I never learn another thing from Titi Yaya, at least this part of my spirit has been awakened. This is oddly comforting to me. I may not be religious, but honoring the orishas seems right for me.

I WALK TITI YAYA back to her apartment so she can rest up. It's been a long few days, and I can see how this asojano healing thing can sap one's energy. If I'm tired, I can only imagine how a viejita curandera feels! On the way over, Titi Yaya tells me I should make an ofrenda—an offering to Yemaya for answering the call.

"What do I need to do to make an ofrenda?" I ask.

"You need to go to the ocean or the river," she answers, as I help her across the street.

Suddenly, I feel a cosmic tug. Sure enough, the water is calling me again.

But Mami would never let me travel by myself to go to the beach. The closest body of water is the East River in DUMBO (the once-run-down-now-trendy-for-millionaires neighborhood, Down Under the Manhattan Bridge Overpass). When we arrive at the café, I call her at home to see if I can take the subway to High Street, which is only two stops on the C train. She tells me yes, but Titi Dolores has to come with me.

Titi Yaya and I go up the kitchen stairs to her apartment. When we get inside, she reaches in the fridge, pulls out some watermelon wedges, and places them on the counter. She then wraps them in foil and hands me the watermelon package.

"Toma. Take this with you. You eat them, then leave the rind for Yemaya at the shore."

"How will she know we're there?" I ask as I put the package in my mini backpack.

"You summon her with this." She presents me with a small wooden rattle. Then she hands me a piece of paper and a pen. "Toma. Write her a letter."

"Uh, what do I say to a goddess?" I ask.

"Thank Yemaya for watching over you. Ask her for wisdom. Then toss the letter in the water."

"OK." I write a few sentences. Then I fold up the note, and put it, along with the rattle and watermelon, in my mini backpack.

"Now, put this on," and she hands me a package of all white clothes. "Es la hora. It is time," she says.

"What's the deal with all the white, Titi?" I ask.

"White means purity. You are entering this religion like a newborn baby. Your old life ends. A new one begins. Now begins your year of learning, your iyaworaje."

I come out of her bathroom feeling awkward, but Titi Yaya is beaming with pride. She adjusts my headwrap, with my curls still poking out from the ponytail atop my head. I am wearing a white sundress but rocking it with my high-top sneakers and my mini backpack. While wearing a dress is not normally my style, I am honored to be initiated like this. I feel like I am going to meet my destiny.

I think about how santería connects me to the history of my ancestors, which goes back all the way to Africa more than five centuries ago. I don't know if I'll ever be a great curandera like Titi Yaya, but I want to learn from her. She is a gift. Her past is my present. Her presence is a present, and I must cherish it for as long as I have her in my life. One day, I'll figure everything out . . . maybe just not today.

I HEAD DOWNSTAIRS to the café, where Titi Dolores, Abuela, and Mami are waiting for me. Mami sees me first, and walks over to me, kissing me on the forehead, and telling me I look beautiful. Abuela grins. Nobody has ever seen me dressed like this before. I suppose it will take some getting used to.

Titi Dolores and I walk to the subway station and hop on the C train for the short ride to DUMBO, the northern tip of Brooklyn, where the East River meets the Hudson River. We walk down the steep hill toward the water.

"Titi, do you ever miss New York?" I ask.

"Every day. My heart will always belong to Brooklyn," she says. "But I'll come back again soon."

"Can you bring Taina and Tommy next time? Please?"

"Of course, Maya. You and Taina need some in-person bonding time."

"Yay!" I really do love all my cousins.

We cautiously navigate the cobblestone streets that lead to a small park right at the water's edge. There are several rocks stacked along the riverbed, so you could step right up to the shore. On a normal day, no sane person would actually dare go into the dirty East River, but today, the water looks calm, clean, and clear blue. There is also a nice breeze that hints at autumn and an always breathtaking view of both the Brooklyn and Manhattan Bridges. I find a nice flat rock to sit on, turn my face toward the sun, close my eyes, and let the sun's rays kiss my face. Titi Dolores finds a rock next to me and sits on it.

"Let me guess: una ofrenda?" she asks, with a knowing grin.

"How did you know?" I reply, agog.

"I was you, many years ago," she says. "Titi Yaya said I had the aché. I was a little younger than you when she was training me, just like she's training you now. But then . . ." she trails off.

"I think I know what happened," I say slowly. "Your grandparents died and Abuela took you and Mami away."

"Yes," Titi Dolores says quietly. "After that, Abuela forbade us to ever speak to Yaya or speak of santería again. I still practiced what she had started to teach me in secret. And I saved the music box that Titi Yaya gave to me. I hid it. It was my only memory of mi tía."

"So, why did you give it to me?" I ask.

"Years later, your mother and I were both pregnant at the same time. I always remembered something that Yaya told us when we were little: that another daughter to be born to the Santos family would be a child of Yemaya.

"You and Taina were about three months apart. You were born first. Taina was a regular, happy baby. But there was something always so serious with you. When you were both about two years old, and we came to visit, I saw you had the aché. Soledad and I gave you two a bath together. Taina would be laughing, content to be playing with her rubber duckies. But you would lie back and float, closing your eyes, as if in a trance. When you opened them, I could see the depths of the ocean in your eyes. So, before we left for California, I gave the music box to you, to tie you to your ancestors. So, you see, this has always been your destiny. You will be the keeper of traditions. You will keep the family together. What you did for your abuela and your titi?"

We are both crying now. After a little, Titi Dolores breaks the sobby silence.

"Well then, shall we do this ofrenda together?" she asks as she dabs her eyes.

I wipe away my tears with my fingers and nod. I reach in my backpack and take out the watermelon. I give one wedge to Titi Dolores and save one wedge for myself. I bite into the sweet flesh and let out a soft moan. The last vestiges of summer taste so darn good. Once we finish eating the red flesh, we each place the watermelon rind by the shoreline.

"¿Lista?" Titi Dolores asks.

"Ready," I say with a brave nod, though I feel butterflies on the inside.

I grab the rattle, wave it in the air, and shake it a few times. Then I take out the folded piece of paper, jump up, take two steps forward, and throw it as hard as I can into the river.

Titi Dolores stands next to me and calls out, "Ori Ye Ye O!"

After a minute, I turn to her and ask, "Is something supposed to happen?"

"I summoned her. Just be patient," says Titi Dolores.

I don't have to wait long to get my answer.

Waves start to form in the river, which makes the water lap up closer to us. I stand up on the rock to avoid getting wet, but that proves to be futile as the waters keep rising. Titi holds my hand tight. Clouds seem to fall from the sky and hover around us. Through the mist, I adjust my vision and see a female figure in the offing. She is moving toward us, arms outstretched. Is it . . . her?

Titi Dolores calls out again, "Ori Ye Ye O!"

Suddenly, a wave of confidence washes over me, and I declare, "I am the daughter of Yemaya, goddess of all living things and the Seven Seas, and my destiny has yet to be fulfilled! I have witnessed the power of the orishas with my own eyes and have been chosen to inherit this legacy. Yemaya, show me the path!"

Then, there she appears—my first glimpse of the Yoruba goddess Yemaya. She is even more beautiful than any portrait imagining her, all seven layers of her white and blue skirts and her long black hair whipping in the wind.

Centuries of Yoruba tradition have led me to this moment, and it is not one that I will ever take for granted. No matter what the winds of change will throw at me, I am keeping my ancestors' culture alive and my family together. I am choosing a destiny that is going to carry me, my loved ones, and our heritage into the future—and it starts right now. Estoy lista.

"Mis hijas," Yemaya says lovingly.

We are her daughters.

And she is our orisha.

My goddess.

THE END

Acknowledgments

First of all, I need to thank my parents, Louis and Virginia Marrero, my life-givers who instilled in me a love of reading, and when I was little, encouraged me to write to my heart's content. (My mom still has every poem and short story I ever wrote. Right, Mom?) To that end, I owe a debt of gratitude for my third and fourth grade teacher, the late Mr. Manthey, for nurturing my obsession for wangling words, pathos, and humor into everything I wrote. I wouldn't be a writer if not for him.

Muchissimas abrazos, besos, y amor a Jaylen, my son around whose orbit I revolve, for being my perpetual inspiration, as well as growing up to be my first consultant and book reviewer. May you always shine bright and let no one dim your light. Again, you are my sun, and I feel so lucky to be your mom. I love you. To my bonus baby, Zoe, thank you for enriching our lives. To Alphonse,

I adore you for being my rock for more than twenty years. Even when the road got bumpy and full of potholes, you nevertheless encouraged me to finish this book and forget the haters along the way. Te amo.

Mucho amor to my own loud and loving Nuyorican family, the Marrero-Carrero-Reyes-Cotto clan, who keep me laughing—and well fed.

This book would not have been possible had it not been for the indefatigable Joy Tutela, my agent. *Salsa Magic* started out as a germ of an idea nearly twenty years ago, with many fits and starts. When life and even basic survival overwhelmed me, I stopped writing altogether. But about once a year, for at least a decade, I'd get a one-line email from Joy asking, "So, how's the book coming?" It was just enough encouragement to get me to reopen my laptop and pick up where I left off—until one day, I had an actual manuscript. Even then, Joy walked me through countless revisions to get the book in pitching shape.

Which brings me to my amazing publishing team and editors at Levine Querido. To my previous editors, Megan Maria McCullough, gracias for taking a chance on me and seeing the vision for Maya and her family; and to Madelyn McZeal, who deftly picked up the baton. Copyeditors never get enough shine, so I'm shouting out Will Morningstar for your thoughtful contribution. A thousand thanks to my current fantabulous editor, Nick

Thomas, whose passionate dedication managed to evoke the best out of me to get *Salsa Magic* over the finish line. And thank you, Arthur Levine, for believing in me.

To the illustrious illustrator, Rudy Gutierrez: I look at this book cover every day and am awestruck by its ethereal beauty. It's more than I could've ever dreamt of. Gracias.

To Mark Wright, my dear friend and soccer consultant, and his lovely wife, Heather, who holds him down and cheers me on: Thank you for guiding me through those action scenes on the pitch.

To my BFF of thirty-plus years, Christina Wolf, who has always seen me as Maya Angelou's "Phenomenal Woman" and a writer, even when I couldn't. Muchas gracias por tu apoyo through all my ups and downs, and for "loaning" me your brilliant daughter Indigo to read an early draft (and for being my first pre-order!).

To my fellow MG/YA authors: Daniel J. Older, for your words of wisdom and encouragement, and to Lilliam Rivera, who, in addition to currently supporting me, gave me my first byline at *Latina* magazine a lifetime ago. Look at us now!

To Robyn Moreno and Michelle Herrera Mulligan, gracias for giving me my second big break, and for your years of friendship— and for introducing me to Joy! And shout out to my comadres in Brooklyn who held me down in those early days of single motherhood: Jamilya Chisholm, Kellie Knight, Kay Wilson Stallings, and Carmen Rita Wong.

To my therapist, Tamia Pleasants, who has kept me sane (mental health is critical, y'all), thank you for helping me transition from surviving to thriving. To my colleagues at Ed Trust, I'm grateful for the stability and peace of mind I needed to be creative again. And where would I be without Cosmo, my cunning Catahoula Leopard Dog, who is a source of constant joy and has prevented me from being a total recluse during the pandemic.

Finally, a huge thanks and much love to my cousins, Andrew and Robert Marrero, for sharing your childhood with me. (And to my Uncle Victor and Aunt Veronica for giving me that opportunity!) Reading you guys book after book all those years ago, you were truly my first audience, and I will always cherish our time together. I'm so proud of the men you've become—but I'll always remember how you showed me that there's nothing like the imagination and wonderment of a child. Now, I get to relish that feeling with kids all over. That's pretty cool.

About the Author

Shala

LETISHA MARRERO has been a writer and editor for more than 20 years across all media and genres. As a culture critic and entertainment journalist, she has written for *Latina* magazine, *The Source*, *Vibe*, *NBC*, *Nickelodeon*, and more. Of Puerto Rican and Black Dominican descent, Letisha hails from New York City by way of Southern California. Mom to a super dope human teenager and a majestic but moody blue-eyed dog, Letisha currently lives in Maryland. This is her first novel.

Some Notes
on this Book's Production

The art for the jacket was first created by Rudy Gutierrez using a digital
layout, then traditionally executed with acrylics and color pencils on
Bristol paper. The text was set by Westchester Publishing Services,
in Danbury, CT, in Goudy, a typeface designed in 1916 by American
Frederic Goudy and revived by Steve Matteson in 2018, endeavoring to be
a lively type with some brush-lettering qualities. The display was set in
Carlton—a typeface with flared serifs and tall ascenders—created by
Letraset Design Studio in 1994, and based off a design from the early
1900s. The book was printed on 78 gsm Yunshidai Ivory uncoated
woodfree FSC™-certified paper and bound in China.

Production supervised by Freesia Blizard
Book jacket, case, and interiors designed by Patrick Collins
Editors: Meghan McCullough, Nick Thomas, & Madelyn McZeal

LEVINE QUERIDO